Part 1
Denial

Chapter 1

Hay Fever

I watched the boys scamper over the gravel and stop at the end of the road. The bus would be here soon to pick them up and whisk them away to school. Erica leaned her head back as she sucked the last of the milk from her sippy cup.

Light filtered through the trees. The shrubs were in full bloom. Days like this always brought me back to my childhood in flashes of déjà vu. It wasn't so much something I saw in my mind's eye but a feeling of happiness, of everything right in the world.

I hiked Erica higher onto my hip as she was beginning to drop. At two years old she was getting too heavy for me to carry, but I did it anyways. It was the feeling of her warm, pudgy little body next to mine.

Elle Klass

Emily Evan's Girls Volume 2

Copyright © 2019 by Elle Klass
Published by Books By Elle, Inc.

ISBN: 978-1-951017-03-3
Cover art created by TL Katt
Editor Dawn Lewis Bookmarks Editing

Author's Disclaimer

This book is entirely fictional. Any characters or events are purely figments of the author's imagination. No one was actually harmed in the making of this story. Many city and business names are fictional as well. No part of this publication may be reproduced, transmitted or redistributed either in its entirety or in part without the author's express written consent.

Books in the Evan's Girls series

Scarlett
Emily
Debbie
Chelsea
Felicia
Chrissy
Eden
Erica

The Evan's Girls Series is based on the children left behind after serial killer Evan O'Conner murdered their families. Each story is about one of his living victims – too young to identify him as a murderer. Too young to even remember their families. They are catapulted into lives that aren't forgiving and some find along the way that they have supernatural gifts.

Emily is a relation of Evan. More about her can be found in the Ruthless Storm Trilogy.

We'd been through so much the months I was pregnant with her I had trouble letting her go now. She was also the youngest. One day they'd all be grown. I pushed those thoughts from my head. That was one day and today they were beautiful young children.

Spring also reminded me of hay fever. *Had I remembered to give Ethan his medicine?* I closed my eyes and ran through the morning's events and sighed relief when it came to me. Right after breakfast. He had the worst case of hay fever I'd ever seen and to make it through a school day in the spring he needed a dose, otherwise I'd have a call from the nurse.

Erica became so heavy I set her down and took her little hand. Together we walked inside the house. I sat on the sofa with my coffee. Erica climbed onto the couch next to me and grabbed a book from the small table beside her. She pushed the pages and pointed, curling her lips into words. "Fi," she smiled up at me with bright, inquisitive, blue eyes. Her tight blond curls needed a brush. "Fi" was her word for fish.

She flipped the next page and repeated the word. I reached for the book in her lap, *The Rainbow Fish,* and opened it to the first page. "Fi, fi, fi," she repeated as I read it.

I read her the story four times before I turned on the TV for her to watch Elmo. He was one of her favorites. "Momo" she called him. Her face lit up in glee and she danced around the room. This gave me time to clean up the breakfast mess in the kitchen.

The boys were getting better about putting their dishes in the sink but Erica had a few years before she could even reach it. Hard pieces of cereal and half a banana lay on the floor below her high chair. I watched my step and leaned over and grabbed the banana. After tossing it in the trash I swept up her mess.

The room grew dark. A single large cloud blotted out the sun but only for a moment as the light returned and spread across the floor. The phone rang, startling me from my thoughts. The caller ID displayed Eric's cell number. Without hesitation I grabbed it off the receiver.

Seldom did he call me. The last time was to tell me he'd been in an accident. Someone had rear-ended him. It wasn't fatal, but trepidation filled me up as I brought the receiver to my mouth. "Hi, honey".

Chapter 2

Mommy Time

A rush of adrenaline pushed through my veins, followed by a sinking feeling in my gut. *Stop it Emily!* I chuckled at myself. If it was a true emergency and something bad happened to him he wouldn't be the one calling.

"Babe," excitement came through in his voice. Not the foreboding excitement but glee. "I just got a promotion!"

The sour feeling fell away and I was excited for him. "That's amazing!" He'd put in for the position but the competition was strong and we crossed our fingers he'd get it.

"Make yourself even more beautiful. I'll be home early and I'm taking the family to dinner tonight!"

It had been hard to shake the fear after the stalker. The mountains, fresh air, and trees helped. They offered serenity and a new start -- a blank slate-- but darkness had taken a resting seat inside me. Every so often it reared its head, but not today. This promotion meant Eric would get a sizable raise and we wouldn't have to pinch pennies so much.

I'd offered to go to work but he squashed it with the cost of daycare. We'd break even and it wasn't worth it. It wasn't that we were poor. The great price we got on the house was a big help but we had to buy a new car because Eric commuted further and the old clunker wouldn't make the drive for long. We paid more each month to get it paid off sooner but still owed several thousand.

I spread peanut butter over a slice of bread and squashed it over the strawberry jelly slice. It was one of Erica's favorite meals. I washed and refilled Erica's sippy cup then entered the living room. "Momo," she sang and danced. She tilted her head and stared at me. "Mommy, mommy, mommy." She grabbed onto my legs and held up her hands. My cue to pick her up.

"Are you hungry?"

She nodded as I lifted her into my arms and carried her into the kitchen. One of the features I loved best about the house. We had a scenic view of the mountain. This time of year, the trees and bushes were so dense I couldn't see my neighbors' homes. It felt as if we were in a world completely of our own.

Lost in the outside world, Erica brought me back to the reality when she chuckled at the squished piece of peanut butter and jelly sandwich she chucked on the floor. I wiped her face and changed her pants then put her down for a nap.

After cleaning the kitchen for the second time I ran a hot bath, poured a liberal amount of bubbles into it, then lit two fragrant candles. I peeked into Erica's room. Her little arms were wrapped around her pink blanket and her tiny chest rose and fell, confirming she was asleep.

I flipped the lights off in the bathroom and eased into the tub as my body adjusted to the temperature of the water. I pushed the button and allowed the jets to blast against my back and sides. The spa tub was my other favorite feature. With three children, I didn't use it as much as I'd like, but when I did I made it count.

I closed my eyes and allowed the bubbles and warmth to take me away. All the worries of daily life vanished and my mind thought of Eric. His soft lips against mine and the gentle caress of his hands over my breasts, tracing a line down my belly. His fingers travelling to my clit and fondling the knob. Desire coursed through me and my breathing became heavy. From the moment I met him I wanted him. It wasn't only my carnal desires and the leaps my libido went through while in his presence. It was all of him. His kindness, level-headedness, his sincerity and trustworthiness, and also his stubbornness and pride. It was everything about him. The whole package and I'd made the pledge to always be his.

I opened my eyes and gasped, bubbles spilled over the tub. I'd added too many bubbles and left the jets on as my mind escaped. I pushed the button off and sighed. I'd have to clean up the mess but wasn't shortening my bath over it. The water was still warm and enveloped me like a cocoon.

I lost track of time, place, and purpose until I heard Erica babble from her room. She would play in her crib for the next few minutes until she got loud, letting me know she wanted out. The scent of jasmine filled my nose and I sighed at leaving my warm, sudsy world. I pushed up and stepped out of the tub. Once I patted dry and smoothed lotion over my body I slipped into a comfortable sundress and dropped my towel onto the bubble mess around the tub.

Luckily the mess hadn't been as bad as it could have been. I tossed the towel into the washer and peeked into Erica's room. She giggled when she spotted my eyes then threw her pink blanket over hers, dropped it and hollered "Pee-boo." I chuckled and we continued the game for a few minutes until she spread her arms and said "Ou," indicating she was done and wanted out.

The doorbell rang. I wasn't expecting anyone and figured maybe it was my neighbor Eilida. We lived so far in the middle of nowhere a run to the store for eggs or sugar took thirty minutes so we'd often borrow from each other.

Erica tagged along beside me as I pulled the door open. A face I didn't recognize stared at me from the other side. His head as bald as a cue ball. His roundish face had a thick jaw and short forehead but his eyes... Something about them lingered at the edge of my brain. A small glint of recognition.

Chapter 3

Hanging

ood afternoon. I work for Nox Pharmaceuticals and we have free packages we're handing out. All it costs is allowing me to do a small demonstration." His lips turned upwards into a smile.

The thing about living in the country is we didn't have a homeowners association and got solicitors from time to time. Usually I didn't open the door. My mistake today. I hadn't even looked through the peep hole, expecting to see my neighbor.

I was ready to politely say "No, thank you" and shut the door, but I was curious. I'd never heard of any company selling drugs door to door. That was odd. "I've never heard of drugs pedaled door to door?"

He smiled wider. "They're not prescription drugs in here." He held up a bag. "Allergy medications -- over the counter."

A little voice in my head reminded me of Ethan's allergies, maybe they had something that worked better than his current medication. The package they were handing out was free. It really wouldn't hurt anything to allow him in and I could always kick him out when he was done. There was no obligation to buy anything today. I relented. "My son has allergy problems. He's ten."

"Safe for children," he assured me.

"Alright, alright come in."

He didn't waste time showing me the products in his bag and giving me a sample kit that included a catalog. Sure enough, they did have allergy medication for children. I'd look into it further, maybe even ask the pediatrician before investing any money. I couldn't shake the strange feeling and glint of something in his eyes that reminded me of... something I couldn't remember. I shook the thought.

As he shuffled around his bag, straightening it out to zip it up, he praised the home, how beautiful it was then asked about our view. We didn't have company much. The occasional cook-out with friends and family but certainly not often enough. The scene from the deck was something I always enjoyed showing off so he hit a button and I decided it wouldn't do any harm. He'd been polite enough and hadn't tried to force a sale as so many others did.

Erica was busy with her toys that were covering the floor where she played. I brought him through the kitchen. I wrapped my hand around the door knob when he said, "Emily."

I'd introduced myself as Mrs. Turnwell and hadn't given him my first name. I was sure of that. *How did he know?* I slid my hand from the doorknob as his voice and my name echoed through my mind. *Had the stalker found me?* From the corner of my eye I spotted the rolling pin I'd left on the table this morning while putting the clean dishes away. I'd meant to put it away too but had forgotten it until now. I stepped backwards, figuring I could grab it, hit him over the head, grab Erica, and run to the neighbors. "Who are you?" I asked, doing my best to stay calm and not alert him.

He smiled, but not the friendly one he'd given me earlier. This time it was sadistic and black flashed across the blue of his eyes. It triggered a fear in me that I hid deep, deep inside. Terror I'd all but forgotten. Flashes of lightning and thunder, creaks in the hallway, and hiding in a dark spot filled with shadows.

"You remember, don't you?" His voice calm.

The perfect spring day became dark as recollection coiled in my brain. "I... I... don't know." It was bubbling in my head, rising to the surface of my consciousness.

"Sure you do." The flashes of black passed over his eyes like the clouds passed over the sun, obstructing its radiance. He moved closer to me and touched my arm, prickles chased up it and the overwhelming urge to vomit hit my stomach. My life rushed back to me. The darkness I'd all but forgotten. The evil that lurked in my earliest memories.

"I'm your brother. I spent years searching for you."

My brothers were kind, loving, protective. Not this man. He wasn't my brother. I didn't know who he was, but his words brought me horror. My gut clenched as I gripped the rolling pin. Bits and pieces of memory drifted across my mind; the police sirens screaming and a set of secure arms carrying me. My mind tried so hard, but I couldn't see a face. I swung the rolling pin at his head. He ducked and lunged forward, pushing me onto the table.

My head stung as it crashed against the thick wood. The rolling pin clattered to the floor.

"Mommy, mommy," came Erica's tiny voice and the pitter patter of her tiny feet.

My baby! I pushed against his bulk to free myself and save my child, but any effort was futile. His chest firmly pressed against mine. I was squashed between him and the table; neither would give.

"Go to your room!" His voice captured a memory that evaporated when a prick stung my neck. Blackness coated the world and my mind sunk into the past, searching for the clues.

Chapter 4

Oh Brothers!

My brother Ray slid his skateboard onto the driveway and coasted to a stop a couple feet from where I sat with my dolls, a ragged ball cap on his head. "Want a popsicle, Em?" he said, lifting his skate board effortlessly with one hand and propping it beside the house.

I nodded. "I want a red one." Cherry was always my favorite.

He ruffled my hair and took my hand as we entered the house. The foyer was a pale yellow, reminding me of warm spring days. Taking off his ball cap he set it on the foyer table and I followed him through the family room into the kitchen where I scrambled onto one of the spinning barstools.

He grabbed a box of popsicles out of the freezer and pulled out a red one, unwrapped it, and handed it to me.

"Thank you," I said and brought the cherry sweetness to my mouth.

Thumps pounded into the kitchen as Mike entered. He didn't do anything quietly. "Where's mine?" he asked, eying me licking on a popsicle.

Ray let out a breath. "You're ten. I don't need to get one for you. Do it yourself." He took a seat next to me and spun me around.

The room swirled around me and I barely saw Mike's eyes deflate as I spun to a stop.

"You always do stuff for her."

"She's four, Mike, get over it." He spun me again.

"Fine," Mike said and reluctantly stalked to the freezer.

The creak of the front door and my mother's voice sailed through the air, "We're home and could use some help, boys."

My chair spun to a stop and I hopped off. In dismay, Mike set his popsicle on the counter on the wrapper. "No one's going to make you put yours down," he said in an angry sing-song voice as he glared at me.

I ignored him and ran into the family room, grabbing hold of my father's leg with my vacant arm. "I love you, Daddy!"

Mike scowled as he walked past me; shivers ran over my spine. It wasn't that Mike ever hurt me. At times he was even my favorite brother as we played *Lego* and *Lincoln Logs* together. He even played *Strawberry Shortcake* with me when no one was watching.

I let go of my father's leg and bounded outside to join my brothers. "Leave something for me," I called, wanting to help.

"You're too small and you have popsicle all over your hands," said Mike as he tugged at a large brown suitcase.

"Who do you think you are *Stretch Armstrong?*" Ray chuckled as he glanced at Mike. "That bag is too big for you. I'll get it."

Ray went to grab the handle but Mike pulled hard enough he and the bag tumbled backwards. He managed to catch his balance and didn't hit the ground.

"Suit yourself," Ray shrugged and grabbed the smaller bag.

"What about me?" I questioned, meeting Ray's eyes and stuffing the popsicle stick into the front pocket of my shorts.

He rummaged in the back of the car for a minute. "You can get this." He handed me a manila envelope.

Happily, I grabbed it and skipped back into the house, tossed the stick in the trash, the envelope on the table, and bounded down the hall to my room.

When I got to my room I remembered I left my dolls in the kitchen. Filled with cheer I skipped down the hall and stopped when I heard my parents and Ray talking.

"He's getting worse. He's totally jealous of her," Ray said.

"He's ten and was the baby for several years. He's still adjusting," my mom said, her voice thoughtful.

"It's been over a year and he's not getting better."

My father cleared his throat. "Family is family. She's a little girl and needed us. We were the best match and she fits so well into the family."

She: were they talking about me? I knew I was adopted and I understood that meant I had another family but something happened to them. A couple years later I learned they'd died. I peered around the corner as if watching them would give me the answers. They stood in a semi-circle facing each other.

My mother, in her warm soothing voice, said, "I enjoy having a girl around the house. Being the only one for so long, it's refreshing." She paused for a moment. "Your brother just needs a little more time. Pay him a little more attention. You'll see."

"Yeah, OK. How's Daren?"

"He's settling in. We helped him unpack, paid his meal card and the rest of his tuition for the semester. I tell you, the price of a college education is an arm and a leg and then some," sighed my father.

Ray shuffled his feet like he did when he had something to say he knew Mom and Dad wouldn't agree with. "Don't worry about me. I'm not going to college. I'm going to intern with IBM and get a job with them."

My mother swished her mouth in annoyance. "That is very competitive. You think they'll want you without a college degree?"

Ray nodded. "You watch!" He turned on his heel and headed towards the hallway.

I scurried back to my room. I hadn't done anything wrong, but sure felt like I did.

Later that night in my room, the shadows danced in the corners. I pulled the covers over my face and scrunched my eyes. The footfalls moved through the hallway and the swirling vortex of sadness and pain swallowed me as I snugged into a ball.

Chapter 5

In the Shadows

I had many nights like that and didn't come out until the sun shone bright through the fabric of my bedspread. Over time they became less until they were gone forever.

Two years later, Ray left us for the internship he promised he was going to get with IBM. He did it. Now he lived on the west coast in San Francisco and here I was still in North Carolina. I missed him every day but it wasn't such a bad thing. Mike finally got over his jealousy of me, instead becoming over-protective.

At the bus stop he'd squint his eyes and glare when someone so much as glanced at me. In public he stayed by my side like if he wasn't there something bad would happen to me. I didn't know what or understand his change of disposition. It was unnerving.

"Go away, Mike." I scowled, grabbing my best friend's hand and getting up from the park bench. It was disconcerting to have him around all the time. He rarely left me alone. Even at the house he had to know where I was all the time.

My best friend, Lori, halted. "You know you're lucky to have a big brother. Why do you get so mad at him?"

She didn't get it. She didn't have any brothers or sisters. "He won't leave me alone."

Lori dropped her eyes. "I wish I had a brother to bother me." She hated being an only child and had always loved coming to my house.

"Come on. We have to go." Mike grabbed my hand.

I twisted it free. "No. We're playing and Mom said to be home by dinner. It's not dinner yet."

He lowered his brows. "There's a man over there by the trees. He's watching you like he plans on kidnapping and torturing you. That's what people do to little girls."

I twisted my head to look.

"Don't look! He'll know I said something and follow us home."

All I caught was a short glimpse of a man in an orange hat. "Fine." I dropped my shoulders. "We have to walk Lori home though first."

"OK, but if he follows us we're going straight home."

The man didn't follow and we made it home safely. I figured he made that stuff up to freak me out.

A few days later, while I was watching Saturday morning cartoons, Mike spent the night at a friend's. I asked my mother a huge question while she was drinking her morning coffee. "What's wrong with Mike?"

"What do you mean, honey?"

"He won't leave me alone."

She chuckled as if what I said was funny. "Now that Ray is gone he has to be the big brother and watch over you. Men are like that sometimes."

I groaned. "I think I liked him better when he was mean."

"Oh honey, the newness of being the only big brother will wear off soon and everything will go back to normal."

The newness didn't wear off. By the time I was ten I knew a thing or two and confronted my mom. "I think Mike needs counseling."

"What?" She placed the rag she was using to scrub the counter down.

"I mean it, Mom. This girl, Kristen, at school, her dad was acting weird and he started going to counseling and now he's better. I want Mike to be better." It was a true story according to Kristen. There was more to the story like how her parents weren't going to get a divorce anymore but I told Mom enough.

She stared at me in shock. "There is nothing wrong with your brother. Give him a break."

I turned on my heel and left the room without another word. They weren't going to listen to me. Parents never took children seriously. They thought they knew everything.

That evening our parents left for a movie and dinner. Since Mike was sixteen they left us alone. The neighbors' numbers were on the fridge in case of emergency.

The doorbell rang. I didn't bother to get off the couch. Mike would have scolded me for answering the door and given me another lecture about the bad people in the world so I allowed him the pleasure. He handed the guy money and closed the door then set the pizza on the coffee table.

I scolded him. "Mom would so yell at you. The pizza's hot and will ruin the finish on the table."

He scowled, mumbled his way into the kitchen, and came back with paper plates and a hot pad. The hot pad he stuffed under the pizza box and tossed a paper plate at me. "You're such a brat."

"Am not!" He was the brat, not me.

"All I do is stuff for you and you complain and tell Mom I need counseling." He dropped a slice of pizza onto my plate. "You see. I'm mad at you and still doing stuff for you!"

"Then stop! I can do things for myself." I grabbed a second slice of pizza and slopped it onto my plate.

The scowl left his face. "Look, when I was your age I guess I didn't want everyone doing things for me either."

That wasn't all of it. Oh no, he wouldn't let me out of his sight. I felt like a prisoner in my own body. "I don't need you protecting me either. OK, nobody wants to hurt me. I have lots of friends and they all think you're weird." That was a lie. They all thought he was cute with his shoulder-length, wavy brown hair and deep brown eyes. We obviously weren't blood-related. My hair was the same shade of pale yellow as the foyer and my eyes were aqua blue.

"There're things you don't know but maybe you should."

"What are you talking about?"

"Remember when Daren visited the summer before Ray left?" Daren was our oldest brother. I didn't know him well because they adopted me a little over a year before he went off to college. Now he was graduated and worked for some big company somewhere.

"Yeah, I remember."

"I overheard them talking. I wasn't trying to eavesdrop or anything." He paused. "Listen, they said something about your," he cringed, "your other family. Before us."

"I don't remember them. Mom and Dad said they died in a car wreck when I was a baby." I couldn't figure out why he was bringing that up. It wasn't important. His parents were my parents. He was my brother.

"It's just," he let out a breath and wrinkled his nose, "they said something about them being murdered and that we had to keep a close eye on you. That the killer would be out soon."

"So that's why you watch me all the time?"

He nodded.

"Listen, I appreciate it. I guess I'm hard on you, but no one is after me. My parents weren't murdered and no one is trying to hurt me." I said that confidently but wasn't so sure I believed the words that came out of my mouth except I'd never felt unsafe. My childhood fear of the dark was over. I was ten and that stuff was for little kids.

Deep inside, in the dark corner that resided in my mind, I knew there was more to his paranoia. I didn't want to hear it so I kept those thoughts squirreled away and told myself he was trying to justify his actions.

He picked up a slice of pizza, folded it, and brought it to his mouth. "Maybe you're right. Listen, I'll ease up on you."

We laughed and joked that night as we stuffed our faces with pizza and watched movies in our VHS player. Half-way into *Dragonslayer* the familiar whine of the screen door caught both our attention. We caught each other's gaze. I swallowed and my heart did a dance.

Mike grabbed the fireplace poker and handed me the little broom. We tiptoed towards the living room. We had to go through a short hall on the left that led to the bedrooms. On the right was the kitchen. I held up the broom in a similar fashion as he held the poker. I stayed behind him. Mike was tall with broad shoulders and could do more damage than me.

The house was a split level, so we had to step down to get into the living room. The room was dark, except for a spill of light from the crescent moon that covered only a small section of the floor. Shadows gathered in the corners. My breath caught and my heart stampeded inside my chest.

"Is that you, Mike?" came a voice from the darkness.

We put our weapons down. The crisis averted. It was Larry, one of Mike's best friends. He lived a few houses over and was known for sneaking through the yards to get to our house. I don't think he ever came through our front door but he always walkied first through the handheld radio device.

"You scared the shit out of Em. What happened to your walky? Batteries dead?" Mike leaned down and pressed his hands against his knees in relief. He'd never admit he was freaked out too. Sure, I could have said something, but being a girl with three older brothers I learned to keep my mouth shut when it came to any of them showing weakness.

Larry flipped the light on, his red hair slicked back. In the past few months he'd started trying to tame his wild mop. I guessed it was to try and attract a female, but hadn't yet worked. He adjusted his eye glasses. The lenses magnified his brown eyes and they always looked buggy. "I did. You didn't answer."

"Shit. It's in my room. Me and Em were watching movies." The words spilled from his mouth, cool and calm.

Larry walked past us into the small hallway. "Look, there's this green truck outside your house. Not right outside but across the street outside. It's been there for hours. I've been watching it and there's a guy in it just sitting there." He flipped the family room light off when we entered it then dropped to his knees.

"What are you doing?" I giggled watching him crawl towards the window.

"We don't want him to spot us. He could be dangerous like a killer or maybe he plans on robbing one of the houses. I don't know. He could even be a spy." He motioned for us to get down. His voice got more excited as he spoke.

Mike let out an aggravated breath. He and Larry had been friends for too many years for him not to listen. "Fine." He dropped to his hands and knees.

They'd also gotten into plenty of trouble together, but this was different. Larry wasn't naturally paranoid like Mike. I dropped as well and followed the two of them to the large picture window. Mike lifted the drape up and we all peered out.

"I don't see it," said Mike.

Larry pointed his finger to the left. "Over there. Do you see it now?"

Mike nodded. "Sure do. Yeah, I don't recognize it."

"I bet our neighbor just bought it or someone is visiting." It was crazy to think anything else and had to have a simple, logical explanation.

"I don't think so. I watched from my bedroom and there's a guy inside it. He's just sitting there." Larry's house had two stories and his room was on the top floor with a view of the road and neighbors across the street.

"You think we should call 911 or something?" asked Mike.

"No!" Larry nearly screamed. "I mean, what are they going to do? This isn't really an emergency. It's not illegal to park your truck and sit inside it for hours."

A shot of bravery coasted through my veins. Before my mind squelched it with common sense, I stood. "I'm going out there. Maybe he's lost or something."

Mike stood and faced me. "Hell, no. You'll do no such thing."

Now I was angry. I wasn't a little girl anymore so I stomped towards the front door. "Yes, I am!"

Mike ran to catch me but I was throwing the door open and running across the street before he could. I heard his footfalls behind me but didn't stop. A spark of bravery and a spark of anger coiled inside me. When I got to the guy I'd ask him if he needed help, maybe even ask why he was sitting outside for hours in his truck. No, I wouldn't be that brave.

I neared the truck and its engine sputtered and caught. It pulled away from the curb and forward onto the road heading toward me. I froze solid. *He was going to hit me!* A hand pulled my shoulder backwards and I stumbled, my eyes on the truck as it rumbled past. The driver's side window was open a crack and a trail of cigarette smoke escaped it. I also saw a glimpse of a dark hat or really dark hair that resembled a dark hat. I couldn't tell which.

That night, my mind drifted to the shadows in the corners. They grew around me as if sucking me in. Footfalls, small but firm, stalked the hallway. I hadn't felt that fear in years but it resided in me that night. I pulled my bedspread over my head and curled into my safe position -- a ball.

Voices woke me later in the night. "She hasn't slept like that for years."

"Should we be concerned?"

"She and Mike probably watched a scary movie."

My parents. They were discussing me. I didn't flip my covers down but stayed in my safe zone and listened.

"Maybe. We have to tell her... one day."

"But not at ten. One day when she is much, much older."

They left. I listened as their footsteps sounded in the hall.

Tell me what? My gut clenched like a hand was squeezing it.

Chapter 6

One of the Guys

Larry ended up sleeping over and the next morning, after breakfast, I followed them to Mike's bedroom. I was part of this and wanted in on the action.

"What are you doing?" asked Mike as I put my hand in the doorway so he couldn't close it.

"I saw it too. The guy almost ran me over. I want in." I stepped forward and wrapped my arms around my chest.

"No way, not after last night!" Mike said in a hard voice.

I figured it was time to be the annoying little sister; after all he was always an annoying older brother. "I'm not going anywhere and if you touch me I'll scream."

"Let her in. We may need a third person anyways." Larry glared at Mike through his thick glasses.

"Whatever," Mike mumbled.

Larry flipped a pocket-sized notebook open. "I wrote down the license plate. Maybe we can get my cousin who works at the license plate agency to get an address and name."

"While you do that, we'll check around the area, look for clues."

I smirked. I knew the young girl who lived in the house where the truck was parked in front of the night before. She was a couple years older but I figured maybe she knew something. "You'll look for clues. The car was parked outside Sierra's house. I'm going over there."

Mike scowled my way but Larry took up for me. "I think it's a great idea.

I walked across the street. There was a small puddle where the truck had been. The way it swirled like a rainbow I knew it was car oil mixed with water. The truck had a leak. I doubted that helped us much as thousands of other cars did too and car oil wasn't unique.

I walked up the steps to her home. There was a small porch with two wicker rockers on it. I buzzed the doorbell. A woman answered, her dark hair tied back in a ponytail and a broom in her hand. "Can I help you?"

"Is Sierra home?"

She opened the door wider and called, "Sierra!"

"I recognize you. You live across the street right?"

I nodded.

"Take a seat, she'll be right down." The woman left me in the room. I plopped onto the puffy green couch and waited. Within a few minutes I spotted Sierra bounding down the stairs, her dark hair bouncing with each step.

"Emily, right?" she asked, a look of confusion on her face.

"Um, yeah." I glanced around searching for her mom. *Was it weird having a neighbor you only barely knew come to your house?* Sure it was, and now it was going to get weirder because I didn't want to take the chance her mom would hear us talking. "Can we go outside?" I nearly whispered.

"Sure." Even her voice held confusion.

Once we were outside she asked, "Why outside?"

It wasn't that I really knew Sierra well. We rode the same bus and spoke on occasion. "Um... Do you know anyone who drives a green truck?"

She chuckled. "I thought something big was going on. My mom's boyfriend has a green truck."

"Does he usually park outside your house for hours?"

"No."

A breeze rustled the trees. "Last night someone in a green truck was parked outside your home and never left the truck."

She lowered her brows. "That is kinda weird, maybe he was waiting for us. We went to my grandma's yesterday." She shrugged like it was no big deal.

"Does he smoke?"

"Yeah, he does. Listen, I have to get back home and help my mom clean the house. Jim is cool. I'm sure he was just waiting for us," she confirmed, I thought more to make herself feel better because there was a touch of something in her voice that told me she didn't exactly like the guy.

We met back up later in Larry's back yard under the shade of the tree line. Larry's cousin took the plate number and said he'd have something for him in a day or two. He wasn't happy about the favor, according to Larry. I figured he had dirt on him and that's why he agreed to do it. Mike didn't find much on the street except the same oil I spotted but he did find something in the woods.

We followed him to the spot. In North Carolina, even in the city, houses were surrounded by woods. We cut through our neighbor's yard across the street and followed the well-worn trail. Mike lifted a branch from a tree and went further into the woods until he came to a tent.

"Someone is living here?" I couldn't imagine why. There were homes on either side and the neighborhood was well-to-do. Not a place vagrants hung out.

Mike swiped the tent flap open. Inside was a sleeping bag. "I don't think they live here. There's no camp set up. Whoever it is just sleeps here sometimes."

Larry crawled inside and carefully patted down the sleeping bag. "Got something," he called. We both peered into the tent. He brought up a camera. A nice 35 mm. "What do you think, should we take the film?" He already opened the back and slid the roll out before we had the chance to answer.

"Careful, you'll expose it," Mike whined.

Larry's bug eyes grew buggier. "I got this."

There was also a trail of cigarettes from the tent to a tree stump. At least twenty butts littered the ground around a stump that was the right size for sitting on. I took a seat but couldn't see much. I wasn't tall enough to see over the little hill, but Mike was the right height.

When he sat he had a good view of Sierra's back yard. It was really creepy to think someone was spying on them. Sierra's father died a few years ago. She and her mom lived alone in the house. Her mom worked at a grocery store somewhere as a manager or something.

"We need to get out of here," Larry said, "before he comes back.' His voice filled with urgency.

I dropped back. "Shouldn't we just call the police?"

Mike recoiled. "No! And tell them what? We found a tent set up in the woods surrounding our neighborhood."

I glared him in the eye and tapped my foot. *Why was he always right?*

"This is creepy, but not illegal. What we're doing is, stealing the camera, so we need to go now!" Larry urged and walked past us toward the trail.

We took the film to the neighborhood store, completed the form and dropped it into the slot. According to the schedule it would be ready next Tuesday.

True to his word, Larry's cousin gave him the name and address of the truck's owner. Filburn Jones, fifty-seven. He lived on the other side of the city.

We came up with a half-baked plan that included binoculars, water, snacks and walkies to stay in contact. Filburn's house was on the opposite side of the tracks from ours. The house was perfectly square, the white paint peeling and cracked from the sides exposing the wood underneath. A Chevy Monza sat on a pile of bricks. It was missing a front tire. A few random car parts were littered around it.

We stayed in the woods across the street from his home, taking turns with the binoculars. We all lied to our parents and told them we were going to McDonald's after school. It was an innocent lie. As we watched we junked on our snacks and sipped the water. It was like a real stake-out. After about an hour with no action, Mike decided to get a closer look. He scurried across the road, hunkered behind the Monza then crept towards the window behind a gnarled grouping of bushes.

A few breathless seconds later the walky squawked, "I don't think anyone's home. I'm going to find a way inside."

"Be careful, Mike." I grabbed Larry's walky with both hands. After several breathless minutes, I turned to Larry. "I don't think we should be doing this. It's dangerous." The clench in my gut squeezed tighter each second that clicked by without Mike getting on the radio.

"Of course this is dangerous, and illegal, but if you're going to do this with us you can't chicken out."

I swallowed. I was a chicken, a big fat yellow one. "Fine."

The walky buzzed finally. "There's no one home."

"On my way," Larry responded. "Take this and call if you see anyone come to the house. You're the look-out."

I grabbed the walky and nodded. Alone in the woods, my mind wandered. Light splintered through the trees but there were still dark corners. A crack from a squirrel jumping onto a dead leaf was as loud in my head as a grown person walking. I pushed down my fear, my eyes shifting every breathless moment I waited for them.

A rustling of leaves caught the corner of my eye. I pulled in my breath and scooted backwards to hide beside a bush. I didn't imagine it. The leaves moved and now footsteps sounded through the leaf clutter.

I clicked the walky and whispered, "Mike, Larry."

It echoed and that's when I stood. "What are you guys doing? Trying to scare me?" I scolded them. Walkies don't echo unless they are close enough and I'm hearing my own voice come through the other radio.

Mike and Larry got a good laugh at my expense. "You should have seen yourself. You scooted behind the bush like a scared bunny rabbit."

"Did not!" I said, to keep my dignity.

They didn't find much in the house but a mess; dishes in the sink, dirty clothes on the floor, an overflowing ashtray and a box in a bedroom closet filled with women's bras. I thought that was extra creepy but Mike assured me guys sometimes did that. At school guys would keep a girl's panties and show them to their friends. He called it an acquisition. I was pretty sure that was more information than I needed at ten. I still thought it was creepy and wouldn't be letting any boys keep my panties, ever. They did learn Filburn didn't live alone because there were two pairs of different sized boots by the door.

Chapter 7

In the Woods

The film came in the next day. We rushed to the grocery after school, unable to handle our excitement as Mike handed the cashier the money. He slid the seal open and pulled out the pictures once we got outside the store. Sierra's yard, Sierra, and her mom. All taken from the spot behind her house.

"This is creepy. We have to tell Sierra. I'm going over there right now with these." I clutched a couple in my hand.

A hand grabbed my shoulder. "What are you going to tell her?"

I glanced over my shoulder at Mike. "About the tent and these pictures. I'd want to know. This is weird and there're a lot of bad people out there." I let the fear show in my eyes for dramatic effect. "Wouldn't you want to know if someone was watching me?" I played on his overprotectiveness.

Mike shifted his eyes and head. "Go." In a quiet voice he followed with, "We'll be watching."

I marched right up to Sierra's front door and rang the bell. Within a few minutes I heard feet then the click of the lock. The door opened. My first glimpse was pink sweatpants and a white T-shirt. "Hi, Emily." Her voice held confusion. I didn't blame her, we didn't know each other well enough for me to be knocking on her door twice in a week's time.

I scratched my head. Now that I was here and she was on the other side of the open door I didn't know how to word it. *Hey someone creepy has been spying on you or you have a pedophile living in the woods behind your house.*

She stared at me expectantly. I handed her the pictures. "We found these in a camera in the woods behind your house." Blunt, but I'd done it. She knew.

Holding the pictures in her hands she studied them, flipping from one picture to the next. "Why would someone take pictures of us?"

I shrugged. "We thought you should know."

"Can you show me where the tent is?"

Shivers ran up my spine. "What if the person is there?"

She scrunched her lips, deep in thought. "I can see the woods from my room. Do you think we can see it from there?"

"Maybe." The house was really quiet. "Is your mom home?"

"No, she's doing inventory tonight and won't be home until early morning."

It was getting late and was almost dinner time. "Why don't you spend the night at my house?"

From her expression and the pause, she thought about it for a minute or so. "No, I shouldn't have even opened the door for you. Those're my mom's rules when she's gone. No one comes over and don't open the door. Which means no one comes in or out."

I was determined. She shouldn't stay home alone not with a creeper in her backyard. "Can I leave you a walkie? Then you can let us know if anything weird happens."

"I have one. Wait here." She bounded up the steps and came back a minute later with a set of Ariel, from *The Little Mermaid,* walkies. She grimaced. "I got these when I was six, but they still work and have good range." She handed me the other one and we set our frequency the same.

It was kinda cool. I had a friend in the neighborhood now too. It wasn't only for big brothers now and all this snooping around was about to get more intense with two girls on the move.

When I returned home, I nearly toppled backwards when Mike and Larry pulled me into Mike's room. Larry closed the door as soon as I was inside.

"What's going on?" I asked, gazing from Mike to Larry.

"It's gone. The tent is gone!"

"Isn't that a good thing?" That meant Sierra wasn't in danger.

Mike paced. "It could be, but what if he's only moved on to someone else?"

I lifted the walkie. "Sierra, come in."

Larry and Mike's brows flattened as they stared at the walkie, then chuckles rose from their throats.

"I like *The Little Mermaid*," I scolded, but they continued.

"I'm here."

"The tent is gone."

The radio wave was quiet for a few seconds then she came back, "That's good, right? He's gone."

"Just keep the walkie close and radio if you hear anything."

"OK."

We ate dinner, went to bed, and awoke in the morning to a sunny day. I buzzed Sierra, she answered, hadn't slept a wink until her mother came home. Every creak, every moan and groan of the house made her tense. I wished she could have spent the night at my house but what mattered was nothing happened. Later that day, after school, Sierra, me, Mike, and Larry took her to the spot we found the tent and the tree trunk. Cigarette butts were still littered everywhere.

She leaned down, picked one up and glanced at me from under a chunk of dark hair that had fallen across her forehead. "Remember when you asked me about the green truck?"

I nodded.

"Jim doesn't smoke this brand. He only smokes menthols. These are regulars." She sat on the tree trunk. "I don't give Jim a chance. He's not my dad but he's not a bad guy either. That truck, it wasn't him. He worked that night."

I guess that meant she'd found it odd too. Having a truck hanging around for hours and a tent in the woods behind her house made her think twice. The good news was that the boyfriend was innocent. The bad news was we didn't know who was the guilty party. We had a full blown mystery to solve.

Two days later, I sweltered outside waiting for the bus. The air was so wet it was hard to tell the difference between it and sweat. At least it was the last day of school and I could spend the hottest days of the year in the air conditioning. The green truck never came back. I stared mindlessly at a school lunch-sized milk carton in the trash only a few feet from me. It made my mind churn. Missing persons. If we could get a list, maybe that would lead us to the creeper. My parents were about to squash that idea and any ideas I had for summer break.

Chapter 8

Larger Than Life

That night our parents dropped the bombshell over dinner. They wanted us to spend a month with a mystery aunt neither of us had met or even knew existed. Mike wore the same question mark on his face that I did.

"No," protested Mike. "You're sending us to stay with some mystery relative. No, you can't do that!" He hit the table with the palms of his hands.

Our father never liked to be challenged. "Yes, we can. We are your parents and you will do as we ask."

Our mom tried her best to wear a poker face, but behind the facade I could tell she was worried. I gave both our parents the best puppy dog eyes I could, pleading 'don't make us'. The fire in my father's eyes flickered for a second then vanished.

Our mother spoke up then, "We know this is a surprise but she's old and doesn't have many years left. She's my aunt and I only recently learned about her. She's my mother's half-sibling and your great aunt." There was something about the tone in her voice, maybe the quiver of it, that made me think she was lying.

I wanted to believe her. She was my mom and never put my life in danger or lied. It would be inconvenient to spend half my summer with a stranger that I was vaguely related to and had never met but would it be the worst thing? No. It would, however, put our mystery on hold. I told Sierra and Larry about checking for missing persons. If they could find a correlation between them and the creepy guy in the house or green truck then maybe there would be enough to take to the police without having to tell about the illegal things we did.

Mike squared his shoulders, fisted his palms and fumed, his gaze shifting from one parent to the next. "I'm finished." He pushed his chair back and turned his back on the table, ready to walk out of the room.

"We wouldn't leave you completely alone with a stranger. We're spending the first weekend there with you and will visit."

Mike clenched his fists tighter until his hands turned red and stomped out of the room. The front door opened and slammed shut. He'd left, probably to Larry's or a walk to settle his anger.

I gulped and dropped my fork. I didn't want to be there either and, after Mike's display, figured I'd go hide in my room. "May I be excused?"

"You too?" asked my father.

"I, uh... it's a lot to think about. It'll be OK. Maybe we'll even enjoy staying with her." It wasn't that I actually thought that but I didn't want to be on my parents' bad side and Mike and I would be together with this unknown aunt. He would never let anything bad happen to me.

"You may be excused."

I swiftly walked out of the room then dropped against the wall to catch my breath.

"They barely ate their dinners," my father said, defeat sprinkled in his tone.

"Put yourself in their shoes. It's a shock and shouldn't be. We've avoided this elephant too long." I imagined my mother and father squeezing each other's hands, because that's what they did when they had to make tough decisions.

It was more than I wanted to hear and didn't understand what my mom meant about an elephant. They spoke as if they'd known this would happen for a long time. *Why would they keep it a secret?*

That weekend, we loaded up the car and headed north into Virginia. It didn't look much different than North Carolina, surrounded in lush foliage and dense trees. Once we were off the freeway we passed through a small town with only one main road.

The storefronts were old, tall buildings with at least two stories. On one corner was a pharmacy that sold ice cream, a grocery across the street, a single gas station with an old time pump, a schoolhouse, and a large church with a brick facade and a tall white steeple.

Several side streets were lined with homes. We drove past them and through the quaint little town, finally turning on a dirt road. It felt like we followed it forever until we reached two tall stone columns multi-colored like bacon. Short, wrought iron fencing wrapped around the property as far as I could see. Thick trees prevented me from seeing more. A sign posted to one column read Hallston Manor.

The road became gravel and we followed it for what felt like another mile or so, then a huge house came into view. It was bacon-colored stone, matching the stone columns. On one side was a white-painted room surrounded with large windows. It over-looked trees and a gentle sloping valley. The front of the house had white columns that supported a small roof over the front entrance. Wrought iron balconies on the second floor jutted beneath white-framed doors.

The left side of the house protruded further than the right and two small windows sat at the highest peaks of the house. Altogether there were nine windows in the stone and I didn't know how many in the white-painted room overlooking the tree-filled valley.

"This is it," my father said, his voice filled with the same awe as I felt inside.

Our house was large with five bedrooms, three bathrooms, a family room, living room, large kitchen including a dining room and a full finished basement but it paled in comparison to this home.

Mike ogled the magnificence of the house, but only for a split second before he painted his angry face on again. He'd let our parents know just how upset he was over this. I was having second thoughts, having a mystery aunt that was rich might not be such a bad thing.

We stepped out of the car and my dad popped the trunk. Before he could lift the luggage out, the front door opened and a stocky man built like a brick with thinning, rust-colored hair came to my dad's side. "No, you go on in. I've got the bags."

My father, gripping one suitcase, dropped his hand and let the rusty-headed man get it. We walked up the gravel path to the front door. Light spread across the foyer from a window above the door and marble floors shone beneath our feet.

We were soon greeted by an older lady. Her silver-platinum hair flowed in wispy loose ringlets from the barrette that clasped them in the back and bright blue eyes the color of mine were set inside soft lines and wrinkles. I'd finally met a relative that resembled me. I knew I was adopted and everyone always said I had my father's cheek bones but they didn't know that was impossible. We weren't blood related. Staring at this woman for a second, I felt a kinship and the feeling that somehow we shared a biological connection.

"Please, it's such a pleasure to finally meet you." She offered a hug to each of my parents and Mike then turned to me and placed her warm hands on my cheeks. "Emily, you are such a beautiful young lady." She gently smoothed the wild ringlets that sprung around my head. Her eyes took on a far away gaze then she snapped out of it. She stood so close I caught the freesia scent of her perfume.

"Forgive me. I'm so happy you're all here. Jessie will bring your bags up." I guessed Jessie was the rusty-headed man. "Caren made lemonade and sugar cookies. We can eat them in the sunroom. The view is relaxing and peaceful." She clasped my hand and we strolled to the white-painted room with all the windows. There were fifteen altogether. Three on each side, and nine open to the full view of the woods.

Warm fuzzies prickled my arms and not from the sun radiating through the glass, but from her, my great aunt. Love, kinship, and belonging wormed its way through my soul and I knew this month wouldn't be so bad.

Mike, though, didn't seem so sure. His eye carried a skeptical look when he noted her taking my hand. He didn't like it, but that was overprotective Mike. Nothing that alarmed me.

Chapter 9

Glad You're Here

That evening, after a large pot roast dinner loaded with carrots, potatoes, and homemade bread, Mike and I headed upstairs to unpack while the grown-ups stayed downstairs. Our rooms adjoined; a bathroom with two sinks between them. More interested in exploring the house, I tossed my clothes into the drawers. They'd wrinkle, but I didn't care. We'd left the doors between our rooms open and I ventured into the bathroom and peeked around the corner. Mike was busy finding places for everything so I sauntered downstairs alone.

The house was huge. A large great room downstairs with a TV bigger than myself, a library with three walls lined with shelves, each loaded with books. The kitchen was separate from the dining room, but still attached, a door between them. The kitchen had two other doors. One led to a garage. It was huge; easily three times the size of ours at home. The other door led to a pantry the size of my bedroom at home with each shelf organized and filled. There was another cozy room with soft velvet furniture and fine china figurines sitting atop tables and shelves.

My aunt, Carly, spelled and pronounced just like Carly Simon the singer she assured us, sat in the sunroom. I didn't see my parents and figured maybe they went upstairs to unpack since they were spending the weekend. Upstairs were several rooms. Most of the doors were closed and I didn't know which room my parents were in so I moseyed curiously through the hallway, listening for the sounds of their voices.

Familiar, hushed tones tickled my ears and I tilted my ear their direction.

"I don't feel good about this. Did you see the way she so obviously pampered Emily?" my mother said in her annoyed tone.

"It'll be fine. Mike isn't one to take jealous and doesn't want to be here. He's made that clear, but I'm glad she agreed to it," my father assured.

I heard a small squeak and imagined one of my parents sitting on the bed. "I know this was the deal, but what do we really know about her?"

"Everything will be fine, but we can't avoid this anymore. My brother was a lowlife, and Philmonia wasn't any better, but Carly isn't like that. She's not," my father reassured.

"We're visiting every weekend and if anything is out of place with either of them we're bringing them home."

My mother was a mama hen who wouldn't allow anything to harm her chicks. I didn't feel anything wrong about the place. Sure, when they first announced this visit to us, trepidation creeped up my spine, but now that I was here and had met my Great Aunt Carly I felt something I'd never really felt and didn't know how to explain. It was like I'd been in the house before, met Aunt Carly before.

My parents had told us they only recently found out about her. It was a long-lost-relative kinda thing, so it was impossible that I'd ever set foot in the house or met her, but knowing that didn't change how I felt.

I had no idea what my father's brother had to do with this. He was dead. I had no clue who Philmonia was and thought it a really strange name. My mind excused that part of the conversation.

That night, in the large bedroom that was mine for the duration of my stay, the shadows in the corners stretched and whispered secrets I couldn't quite hear. I curled into a ball beneath my covers. The whispers didn't stop but chattered incoherently above the comforter. Footsteps in the hall pounded the floorboards into my room. A coldness crept under the covers and slithered up my spine. I snuggled closer into myself then a flash lit up the room and a crash rattled the house.

I threw the covers off and ran through the bathroom into Mike's room, never taking a glance at the shadowy corners. Without hesitation I jumped into his bed.

"What's wrong, Em?" He rolled over onto his side, bunching the pillow beneath his head so he could get a full view of my face.

"The house is creepy at night."

"It's like a storm at home, Em, nothing to be scared of. Look, you take the bed and I'll sleep on the couch." Light flashed outside, lighting his room for a moment. There was nothing out of place, no monsters or ghosts in the corners. The room looked the same as it did during the day. Then the light went dark and thunder roared.

"You don't have to do that. This is your room."

He smiled. "You're my sister and you're scared. It's my job to take care of you. In fact, I get the feeling that's the only reason I'm here. You keep the bed." He sat up, grabbed his pillow, and padded to the couch. "Good night, Em."

"Good night Mike." I watched his chest rise and fall in the dark through the flashes outside as the storm moved on. I thought about his words. His idea that he was here to take care of me. It put me at ease. "Mike?"

"Yeah, Em. What is it?"

"I'm really glad you're here."

"So am I." Rain pounded against the window but I still heard his quiet words.

We woke in the morning to sunlight streaming through the window and birds singing their summer songs. The shadows in the corners were gone, replaced by the concept of a good day ahead.

The breakfast table confirmed my positive thoughts. It was like a smorgasbord with fresh cantaloupe, strawberries, and grapes, with eggs, toast, and bagels. To drink was orange juice and milk. *Did my aunt always eat this way?* I wondered as I loaded my plate.

My parents left the next morning after breakfast leaving us alone with Aunt Carly. Mike felt more at ease since she was really nice. We spent that day swimming in her giant pool behind the house and ate barbecued bacon cheeseburgers and homemade fries for dinner followed up with banana splits. I thought my gut was going to split after eating so much. She called it a wholesome American meal.

I even grew used to my room at night, so long as the storms stayed away. After about a week, she took us to the city for a movie. She claimed it was the closest movie theatre. We rode in a sleek cream-colored Mercedes Benz and a chauffeur drove.

"How did you get all this money?" I asked in curiosity. The leather seats were soft and comfortable. Trees whizzed by as the car glided over the freeway.

Mike elbowed me and gave me the 'that's rude' look, but I ignored it.

Aunt Carly chuckled. "My late husband. His family owned all the land the town was built on. Old Southern money. When he passed, I inherited it. There wasn't," she paused for a moment that passed so quick I almost didn't catch it, "anyone else for it to go to."

Mike spoke up then, "What about your kids?"

"Oh, I wanted several, enough to fill up that huge house, but we couldn't have any."

"I'm sorry." Mike's eyes darted away from her to the window in shame.

"No, no. It's OK. I had a niece. She looked so much like you, Emily, with blond springy locks and bright blue eyes but her father..." She switched gears. "We're here!" She clapped her hands in excitement.

The movie theatre and city were far more modernized than the one horse town she lived in. I felt at home. There were fourteen cinemas and the place smelled like buttery, mouth-watering popcorn. She bought us each an extra-large popcorn and slushies. I got the red and Mike the blue. We watched *Gremlins 2*. After the movie, she took us out for pizza. I ate so much that summer, I was sure I'd get fat.

Chapter 10

Skeletons

Over dinner one night, Mike asked Aunt Carly the oddest question. "What's in the room with the pull down steps?"

"An attic, nothing up there but memories," Aunt Carly said as she finished salting her dinner.

"Of your husband?"

I was ready to give him the 'that's rude' look. He stuffed a bite of steak into his mouth and expectantly awaited her response.

"And other things of my past." She glanced at him. "I have a surprise for you."

He narrowed his eyes. "You do?"

"Eat up and I'll show you."

For someone who fought the idea of visiting for a month he shoved the food into his mouth now with urgency.

I chuckled and he gave me a sideways glance. Carly winked at me. After dinner she brought us into the garage.

"Your parents tell me you got your driver's license in May," she continued as she walked towards a sporty red Pontiac Fiero. "This little car has been sitting here. I rarely drive anymore. It hardly has any miles on it..."

She continued talking as the anticipation rose in Mike.

"And your parents agreed that I can give it to you. What do you think?"

Mike's eyes grew wide in excitement. "They did?"

Daren and Ray got cars, clunkers, nothing like this bright Red Fiero. My parents said they needed to learn responsibility and an older car would teach that.

Aunt Carly sighed. "It only has two seats so I'll have to sit this one out, but I bet Emily would like a ride. The keys are under the visor."

He rushed to the car and opened the door. I ran to the other side and sat on the soft fabric seat. The car looked brand new and, like she said, when he dropped the visor keys dropped into his lap.

The garage door lifted behind us and he started the motor up. It purred like a new car. It even had the new car smell. Mike unrolled the window and leaned out. "Thank you, Aunt Carly."

A smile spread across her face and she waved. "Have fun and don't stay out too late."

Mike took it easy on the gravel road so as not to scratch the car. He fiddled with the buttons and gadgets. Everything was electric and motorized. He was a boy with a new toy. I knew that look and everything that went with it. With three older brothers there wasn't much I didn't know about guys.

We made it to paved road. The wheels of the car zipped over it and wind rushed through the windows.

"This was really nice of her," I said. He'd been skeptical, but he couldn't deny now how awesome Aunt Carly was.

"Yeah, I guess. I mean she didn't have to give me a car." I heard an unmistakable hint of cynicism in his voice.

"This isn't just a car. An old Pinto or Honda hatchback would be just a car. No, this is a sportscar. It'll get you the attention of every girl in school who isn't already after you for your charm." That was a hit on his personality but he'd get over it.

"It is nice and drives smooth, hugs the corners." He paused for a second. "Did you notice though how she used this to change the subject at dinner?"

"I guess. You asked her a goofy question anyways. Most people keep crap in the attic. Have you ever looked in ours?"

"There's something there. I sense it. It's the way her lip curls in the corner when she smiles. Your lip does the same thing. The way she flips her hair back. The way she makes me want to believe her. It's all like you."

"What exactly are you saying, Mike?"

"Look, we never knew about her. Suddenly we have a new aunt and she's richer than Midas. Doesn't it seem suspicious to you? Like, maybe... Never mind, it's silly."

I hadn't thought of it exactly the way he had. I was more of an optimist and liked to believe the best in every person and situation. Mike was always paranoid. "It's not silly. What were you going to say?"

"Mom and Dad adopted you and I don't think they knew anything about your biological family. If they did they've never said and I just think, maybe, Aunt Carly is your aunt by blood."

To keep my life copacetic I denied any such thoughts. "I don't think she is. Everyone has a twin. Mine is a lot older. That's all."

He shrugged. "Could be, but we're still going up there."

I straightened my back. "Don't involve me. You can go alone."

A few days later, he woke me in the morning, early as the sun was rising. "She left on her walk. Quick we only have about an hour."

I rubbed the sleep from my eyes as he reached for my hand. "Come on. I want to show you something."

He dragged me down the hallway and pulled the ladder. I couldn't believe I was doing this. It felt like a betrayal. Then his words sunk in. "Wait, you've already been into the attic?"

He didn't respond as he lowered the door. Light shone through the small round window, settling on the dust.

"Over here." He motioned for me to join him. He sat on a box and grabbed a photo album. "Look."

I grabbed it from him and glanced through it until a picture caught my eye. "What's she doing with a picture of me?"

"That's not you, Em. Look at the film. It's yellowed. That picture is old."

I pulled it out of the sleeve. The back said something that was too worn to distinguish. "Maybe it's her when she was a baby."

"I don't think so. Look at the clothes and the white baby shoes. That's '70s style."

He had a point. "Maybe it's the niece she talked about. The one with blond ringlets and blue eyes like me."

He shrugged. "Yeah, could be."

"It's weird though, Mike. I'm not blood related to any of you, yet I feel like I am sometimes and this picture really looks like me."

"I told you I thought you and her were blood and you also do look like Dad. You could be his blood child."

"No, I don't. People say that and you all agree only to make sure I always feel like part of the family."

"Em." His eyes penetrating mine. "Blood or not, you are part of the family and when we get home I'm going to show you pictures of Dad at your age. You do look a lot like him."

I flipped through more pictures, then closed the album shut. A cloud of dust tickled my nose. When I sneezed the album fell. I picked it up to place it back in the box and something dropped from it and slid along the dusty wooden floor. Another picture; but not of the same girl. It was more recent. Three children; a baby girl who looked barely able to walk, and two little boys. The larger boy's eyes appeared to change, to watch me from the across the film. A black cloud moved over them and I dropped the picture.

"Em. She's on her way back. We need to get out of here." He stood in front of the round window, his eyes fixed below.

He didn't have to tell me twice. The little boy in the picture spooked me enough that I was at the stairs before Mike.

My biological family was dead and knowing anything about them wouldn't bring them back. I was content in my life. There was no reason to dig skeletons from the closet. All I'd get was a bag of mismatched bones.

Chapter 11

The Lake

Like clockwork, the next morning Aunt Carly went for her morning walk. I wasn't an early riser in the summer but was curious, especially after Mike said she went every morning. *Where did she go?*

I stayed a bit behind her, allowing her into the woods before I started on the trail. The trees were dense but the trail was free of debris, making it easy to stay quiet. I felt as though I was spying on her or something bad and reminded myself Aunt Carly was nothing but amazing.

Even though it was the middle of summer, the air was chilly and a low fog arose from the ground the further into the forest I followed, always keeping her platinum-silver hair in sight. I dipped back and slipped behind a bush, when out of the trees arose a clearing. The fog was much thicker and crested a lake. She sat on a carved wooden bench.

"You should join me," she said, not looking my way.

How did she know I was here? I slunk from behind the bush and came to her, taking a seat next to her. She had her feet stretched out; her heels resting on the dirt and toes in the air.

"My husband and I used to come out here every morning. It was our special place. The lake is fed by an underground spring so there's fish and other wildlife."

She didn't talk much about her husband or any family. The only photos she had were in the attic. At that moment it struck me oddly. Most people had pictures of family all over the house but not her. "You miss him. Is that why you don't have any pictures hanging?"

She turned her head, her eyes meeting mine. "When you get to be my age it's not about the past but the present and what's left of the precious future."

That statement was so profound. I was still really young and had nothing but the future. Her life was mostly in the past. I thought of my brief past and how good my life had been. *Had hers not been so good?*

She turned her head to gaze at the lake once again and reached out and grabbed my hand. "I'm so happy I've had the chance to get to know you and Mike. I wasn't so close to my own family and left home at sixteen. It was a struggle. A few years later I met the man of my dreams and he swept me off my feet and brought me here."

The distance between us became closer and no more words needed to be spoken. The trees around the lake mirrored on the water's surface making it look as though the trees were never-ending. It was serene; like a really good dream.

Later that day, Mike and I were in the pool like we were most every day. My light freckled skin was now a light brown from all the sun and Mike, who had darker skin tones than me to begin with, was a much darker shade of brown. My blond hair was platinum. We hit the beach ball back and forth for several minutes until it bounced out of the pool.

"I'll get it," I called and ran after it as it rolled across the patio onto the wooden deck. I reached down to grab it and a small wind gust caught it and carried it over the pool deck to the ground below. It rolled. I scrambled off the deck, down the steps, and finally caught up to it resting beside the house. With the ball in my hand I saw something there I'd never seen before. Neither of us had been below the deck until now. Sun shone from the slats in the deck onto windows. Curtains covered them and I couldn't see in but was sure it was a basement.

We'd been here for almost three weeks and for the first time I was realizing there was even more to the house than I'd previously thought. I clambered the steps and found Mike standing beside the pool.

"Where did you go?" he asked, a towel in his hand.

"To get the ball." I tossed the ball in and jumped in after it.

Once he'd jumped in I cozied up to him and whispered, "I found something."

His eyes narrowed. "Like what? A snake?"

"No silly. There's a basement."

He chuckled. "Don't you think we'd have noticed a door to it by now? We've explored every room in the house."

"No, we haven't."

His eyes glanced upwards as he thought about that statement. "Aunt Carly's room. But it's upstairs. There wouldn't be a staircase from her room into a basement."

"Well, then where?"

"Let me think about it." He pushed off from the side of the pool and floated backwards.

"Well?"

"I'm thinking." He caught up to the ball and threw it my way. "Catch!"

I hit it back to him. It wasn't until later he brought it up again. "When she goes for her walk tomorrow morning we'll check her room. This house is so fantastic that maybe the door *is* in her there."

The next morning Mike woke me up with a start. "Let's go," he said.

Sleepy-eyed, I rose from the bed and followed him to Aunt Carly's room. It was huge with a sitting room that included its own couch and big-screen TV. Through a wide archway was her bed. It was the biggest bed I think I'd ever seen, even bigger than our parents' bed. She had twin walk-in closets that were like rooms. Inside the bathroom were double sinks, a round tub that looked like a hot tub, a separate shower, and another big closet. We didn't see any doors anywhere.

"It's not here," I said, ready to leave her room.

"It's gotta be." He doubled back to her closets and shifted around them, pushing clothes.

"She'd going to notice things are out of place."

"I'll push everything back. She'll never know."

I remembered how she'd noticed I was following her. She was

far more perceptive than he was giving her credit for. I sighed and stepped into another closet. I was small enough I stepped between the clothes and stood behind them, and that's when I saw it. "Mike, here. I found it."

Within a moment he joined me. We stared at the door knob for a minute before he swallowed. "Ready?" he asked.

I nodded and he twisted the knob. The door creaked open into darkness. He felt for a switch on the wall. I stepped back and searched inside the closet. Some rooms had light switches on the outside and this one did. I found it only a foot or so from the door and flipped it.

We crept down the steps carefully, purposefully. Dust swirled around us and tickled my nose, making me sneeze. The steps didn't go straight down but stopped it the middle on a landing and went in the opposite direction until we reached the bottom. Mike took the first step off the stairs and a light above his head turned on, followed in synchronous action by several ceiling lights. They were like dominoes falling. The room seemed to go on and on.

I expected to see an unfinished room with cement floors and wires hanging between two by fours in the walls, but I didn't. The floors were covered in hard wood and the walls were painted a cream color. Old furniture and a couple chests was all the basement housed.

"This place is huge," Mike noted, his eyes moving over the large space as he took it in.

There were no walls separating rooms. I walked forward first in wonder, gravitating towards an old desk with a roll top. There was a sewing machine in a wooden case. It had to have been a really old model. It said *Singer* on the side. I grazed my finger over the top. The furniture was mostly made out of intricately carved wood. It looked centuries old.

Along the wall a sheet covered awkward-appearing furniture, but when I lifted the sheet off it displayed a white wooden cradle with rounded feet that made it rock. Next to that was a matching dresser and changing table. "Didn't she say she never had children?" I asked Mike.

"Yeah, she said she wanted some though, then she talked about her niece. Why?" He was sifting through an old chest.

"Because this is baby stuff here."

He turned his head and glanced my way. "It sure is. You think maybe she lied and they had a baby? Babies used to die during birth."

I shrugged. "I don't know. Maybe."

"Take a look at this," he said, holding an open folder in his hands.

I joined him. "What is it?"

"Court papers." He sat on the couch next to the chest and a cloud of dust lifted off the cushion and tickled my nose. I sneezed again.

I glanced over his shoulder to read but didn't get a very good view.

"I think they tried to adopt her niece, Philmonia, but according to these papers it wasn't granted since both of her parents were alive and able to provide for her." He continued reading. I listened.

"Child protective services were called but after an inspection they left Philmonia with her parents."

I went back to the chest and dug around more. At the bottom were newspaper clippings. I pulled them out and started reading. There was a man; his green eyes stared at me from beyond the page. They penetrated inside of me like needles. I dropped the paper and it floated toward Mike.

"What's this?" he asked as he picked it up. He studied it for several minutes, his jaw slack.

"What is it, Mike?"

"This man. He did really bad things to people, including his own daughter. The things he did are so bad I can't even tell you."

I didn't need to know the awful things he did, but I was curious about his daughter. "How old was she?"

"A teenager at the time but the things he did to her went on for years. He tortured her in ways that are... immoral."

I gulped hard. "What do you mean?" *Wasn't any torture immoral?*

He twisted his lips as he searched for the correct words. "He umm... he did things, he touched her and more in places of her body he shouldn't." He stumbled over the words, searching for a nice way to say something really bad. There was no nice way to say it.

"He violated her."

His eyebrows went straight across like a pencil. "How do you know that? You're only ten."

"I listen when Mom and Dad watch the news sometimes. There're all types of bad things the newscasters talk about." I glanced into his eyes, they widened as I spoke. "He did more than violate, he raped her didn't he?"

He nodded.

We continued searching through the chest and all the little secrets Aunt Carly had hidden away. The child they tried to adopt, the bad man, and more. Most of it though wasn't all that interesting but it did date back a hundred years and kept mentioning the name Hallston. We figured it was his family. A record of how they made and spent their fortune.

We got lost in the memories of the clandestine room until we heard the door open.

Chapter 12

What Happens at Aunt Carly's Stays at Aunt Carly's

My heart pushed into my throat. We were so busted. Both of us stared at her, speechless. We'd been caught with our hands deep in the cookie jar.

Slowly she crept down the steps, her hand on her chest. "You gave me a good scare when I couldn't find either of you anywhere. I thought I'd have to call your parents. That wouldn't go over well. What are you doing down here?"

"We uh... well..." Mike stammered.

When she got close enough, her eyes shifted from the uncovered baby furniture to the open chest. She sighed. "I guess you probably have a lot of questions and if I don't answer them you'll talk to your parents."

"We wouldn't do that." I shook my head.

"It's OK." Dust plumed around her as she took a seat. "You have to promise me one thing."

We stared at her, wide-eyed, nodding. "OK."

"Anything I tell you, you can never repeat. What you learn at Aunt Carly's stays at Aunt Carly's."

I lifted my pinky to her. "I pinky swear."

She smiled and curled her pinky around mine then Mike offered his.

"Well, when I was a girl my family wasn't like yours. My parents weren't like yours. I had a twin brother but there should have been three of us except one died in utero." She spotted the question mark in my eyes. "Before birth. My brother wasn't such a bad kid at first, but my parents were really bad to him. They did mean things and one day he got really mean. That's when I left. It was years later when I learned that he had a baby girl, Philmonia."

I recognized the name from the court papers. Her niece, the one she spoke to us about.

"She was cute as a button. I visited my brother and his wife, thinking maybe now that he was in his own home, with his own family, he'd be a good man. At first when I started coming around he was, but over time I began to see it. The same evil I'd seen in him as a teenager. It had changed though and he vented his anger through his family. His wife feared him and all I could think about was Philmonia. What kind of life would he provide for her? There was nothing good left inside him. It was stolen during childhood."

I swallowed. "But you turned out OK."

She smiled. "It took me a long time to heal, but the things they did to him were worse because he was a boy. In those days people didn't expect much from girls, so my parents ignored me and pushed all their rage onto him." She paused.

"My husband went behind my back and offered him a boatload of cash. Of course, my brother didn't turn down the money. He took it with a promise to let us adopt Philmonia then switched his mind at the last minute. I was so angry, angrier at my husband. He wanted to please me, but should have spoken to me first. After that, allegations were made and child protective services were brought in. They didn't find anything to warrant taking Philmonia from her parents. My brother cut me off from her and I fought, spending thousands and thousands of dollars to even get visitation. I got nothing. Many years later, when Philmonia was a teenager, he was caught committing violent crimes against underaged women. Those crimes included sexual assault of his daughter."

That moment the air was completely still; the air didn't blow from the vents, the lights didn't buzz. There was no sound. I understood now why our parents didn't want us to visit. They were afraid Aunt Carly was like her brother, but she wasn't. She was nothing like that and always treated us good.

She reached for the newspaper clipping. The one with the man with the eyes. "That's him. After he went to prison, her mother committed suicide."

"What happened to her? Did you finally adopt her?" Mike asked in a tone that said he knew the sad answer.

She shook her head. "No. I tried, but she was so full of hate she wanted nothing to do with us. The state placed her in foster care. Eventually she ran away."

"What happened to her?" I asked. My guts twisted inside. She needed a home and love.

"Eventually she made contact with me. It was several years after, but she did. She'd been married and they had a child. A boy. All I ever wanted to do was help her, so I gave them the money for a down payment on a house. They had two more children, another boy and a very sweet little girl." She ran her fingertips through my curls.

It sounded like things turned out for her. I couldn't figure out why tears were falling from Aunt Carly's eyes. "What's wrong?"

She sniffled. "They were killed. Someone broke in to their home and..." She cupped her face in her hands.

"Don't cry, Aunt Carly." I wrapped my arm around her and buried my face into her arm. I didn't want her to be sad. "You have us."

She raised her head and lowered her hands. "I do, and I'm so thankful I do and that you have such wonderful parents. They love you so very much."

We left the room and the memories, locking them away where we should have kept them. I didn't enjoy seeing Aunt Carly in tears because we brought back the pain. I also never told my parents what she told us and neither did Mike.

Chapter 13

Solving a Crime

Our parents showed at Aunt Carly's to bring us home, but since Mike had the Fiero he followed them home. I rode with him. The little car seemed to just fly over the road. We didn't talk much about Aunt Carly's instead our minds adjusted to the thought of being home and centered on what Larry and Sierra learned, if anything.

The next day the four of us met at Larry's house. Between him and Sierra they recounted their steps and what they had learned. They started with my idea of finding all the missing persons in the area by going to the library and sorting through the newspapers. By the time they were nearly through they realized they didn't know how they'd be able to find a connection between the creepy guy who owned the green truck and the missing people, so they worked another angle. He had a fetish for women's bras so they started looking for crimes that included bras.

It was really weird to think about, but they started finding stuff when they went outside our local area. They found an article from Virginia about a murder victim who was found braless. In South Carolina the same thing and the women looked almost identical. They found a second one in South Carolina, almost the same. All the crimes happened within the past five years, which gave them another idea.

They found public records on the man with the green truck -- Filburn Jones. According to the deed he'd lived in that home five years and four months. They had no idea where he lived before that, but all three of the murders they found occurred within a 150 mile radius. He showed us on a map. Filburn lived smack in the middle.

Larry's face harbored a straight face. "We decided to start looking elsewhere." He paused for a second. "On the west coast."

Knots tightened in my stomach as I expectantly awaited what he would say next.

"We found more similar murders in other states; Seattle, Oregon, and Montana." His expression didn't change as he studied our faces.

"Holy shit! He's a serial killer!" Mike spat.

"Yes but there's more," said Sierra. "This happened eight days ago."

She handed Mike a newspaper article. I peered over his shoulder and gasped once I finished reading.

Filburn Jones died in a car wreck. He was killed by a drunk driver. I sat back to get my breath. *What kind of dumb luck was that?* "What did you do?" I asked.

Larry shrugged. "Nothing, he's dead."

"Someone else lived with him." Mike reminded.

"Yeah, but the house is vacant now. Whoever it was is gone. Since the wreck happened in the green truck we figured it was him out here that night and the tent--"

I cut Sierra off. "But you don't know for sure?"

"No, but what else can we do?" she answered my question with a question.

Mike studied their faces. "We go to the police."

"We thought of that and we even found a residence belonging to Filburn Jones in Idaho. That points to him being the killer, not anyone else," Larry reasoned.

"I guess," was my response. It had been exciting more than scary, but most of all Mike and I worked together along with friends. Together we solved a crime and it would be nice to be recognized as juvenile sleuths. On second thought, our parents might get a bit upset, so maybe it was best to let it rest.

Part 2
Revelation

Chapter 14

Stunk Like Skunk

The next few years flew by and before I knew it Mike was in college and I was in high school. It was there I met my first boyfriend, if I could call him that. He was hot in a bad boy way; long hair, beat up holey jeans, T-shirt, and facial scruff. He didn't just wear grunge. He *was* grunge and a good likeness to the legendary Kurt Cobain.

He was a junior and I nearly toppled over myself the first day he gave me a half-cocked, sideways upper-lip-lift smile in art class. After a few more on consecutive days I was jelly, so when he pressed his back against my locker between first and second periods I stopped everything and, controlling the drool, listened. Like a puppy I followed him as he suggested we skip the day and hang out at his pop's house.

My gut instincts said *No, don't do it.* I heard Mike's voice in my head, *He's no good and nothing you want will come out of this,* but I swished it away and went anyways. His pop's house was a simple ranch-style brick home. Through the front door were a worn tan carpet and a mismatched set of orange and green chunky couches. The coffee table was a huge bulky block of wood cluttered with an overflowing ashtray, opened pizza box with a day or so old slice of everything, and several empty beer cans. By the looks of it he wasn't finicky about the brand so long as it was domestic.

"Get comfortable," he said and left me staring at the furniture, wondering what he meant.

Get comfortable as in strip down comfortable or take a seat on the couch, watch for the empty beer cans stuffed between the seats comfortable?

He returned with two beers. "Catch," he said, pretending to throw it.

I put my hands out and turned my head waiting for the toss but it didn't happen.

"Kidding. Here." He popped the tab and handed me the beer.

He wasn't much for speech and long conversations. The beer was disgusting and I sipped slowly.

He pulled something from under the couch. "You smoke?"

No, I didn't, but my brain and mouth weren't in the same place. I nodded my head yes. He lit it, took a long drag and inhaled. After a couple minutes he let it out.

"You don't look like a girl that's smoked before. Do what I did."

I took the joint and sucked it in then held it in as long as I could before my lungs complained and the smoke came pouring out.

"No worries, you'll get used to it."

I didn't want to get used to it. The smoke stunk like a skunk and my lungs felt as though something was scratching them. This wasn't my thing but for the moment with him I craved the wild side of life.

He turned on the stereo and music filled with anger and hard beats consumed the air between us. He wrapped an arm around my shoulder and pulled me towards him. I wasn't sure what was happening or what I should do. Every muscle in my body tensed tight as a rod.

"Relax. Take another hit." His advice to get me loosened up, but I didn't think it would work.

I'd spent my life protected by older brothers, mostly Mike, and now with none of them around I was walking the rope between the good me and the bad me. "OK," I squeaked as I lifted my hand for the joint. Instead he grabbed my face and blew his smoke into it. I coughed and squinted my eyes as the smoke passed.

"This time when I blow you breathe it in, suck it into your lungs." He took another drag and the cherry lit bright red burning the paper and pot inside it. He blew it into my face and, like the obedient child I was, I sucked it in. It was a bit smoother this time but I still choked and gagged. It was enough for me to grab the beer and take a large gulp. I nearly gagged as the cool liquid slid down my throat.

Soon my mind was somewhere else. Reality was fuzzy. His fingertips brushed over my nipples through the fabric of my bra. Tingles ran up my spine but I felt paralyzed in the moment. How they got there I can't remember, but soon his fingertips were climbing up my abdomen and around my breasts then cupping them beneath my bra which was shoved over the developing fullness of my chest.

I took in a deep breath. Fear, delightful sensations, and a voice in my mind telling me to flee coalesced in that dark moment as my body froze. His lips traced my neck, landing on my lips, while one hand cupped a breast and his other slid down my pants with ease. I was helpless as his finger rubbed against my clit, sending deep, lustful desire throughout my body.

Mike's voice in my head shouted at me to leave. Shouted I had no business with this guy but I couldn't do anything. My body and mind were putty for him.

"Now you're loosened up," his voice sultry in my head. He grabbed my hand and placed it over his hard member, moving it up and down. The movements became quicker. "Like that. I'm moving my hand."

Following his directions, I continued to rub his swollen member as his fingers rubbed against my clit and rubbed the area between my pussy and leg. I wanted something I wasn't ready for. He knew that and moved my hand then brought me on top of him, my panties the only thing between his enlarged cock and my very wet vagina.

The urges in me drove me to push against him, rub along his length until a new sensation rocked my body. It felt like nothing I'd ever experienced. I dropped my head back and rubbed against him faster until the lustful sensation eased. As if in a tube, I heard him moan.

I faced him. A smile across his face. "God that was good." I glanced down to see a creamy puddle dripping between the tip of his groin and belly button.

My first sexual encounter. I'd never forget. By the time I got home that afternoon I felt both unclean and excited. The diversity of my feelings drew me towards him. It was something I needed to understand. *Was what we did dirty or was it Mike's voice in my head that made it feel that way?*

I showered, scrubbing my body vigorously. I reminded myself several times what we did wasn't dirty. It was normal. I was in high school and for the first time unprotected from brothers who, if they had their way, would never allow me a boyfriend. I really wasn't reminding myself but attempting to justify my actions.

Dennis didn't make it to school the following day or the next. I was relieved yet torn. I didn't understand what that day meant, what we did meant, if it meant anything. To me it was big. I'd done something that was now embarrassing, trashy, and unlike me.

The third day he appeared by my locker about midday. I glanced at him as I shoved a book into my locker and took out another. I didn't know what to say, *Hi, glad to see you again?* Or give him a kiss or cuss him out for not bothering to call or anything. As my mind contemplated all the dorky things that might flow out of it I noted he carried no books. He never had any books on him. I decided on, "Hi, Dennis."

His dirty blond hair was pushed to the sides, uncovering his blue eyes. He stuffed both hands into his front pockets. 'Nobody calls me that except a few teachers. It's D."

"Hi, D," I restated. I didn't really know what to say and was nervous in his presence even though I desired him near me.

"There's a big party tonight. I want you to meet me there."

Did that mean I was his girl? This was a guy that I got the impression had a lot of "friends" but not real and true friends. People thought he was cool. "Sure," the word left my mouth before I was done contemplating it. My mind cringed but I couldn't get out the words to turn him down even though I knew this was over my freshman head.

"See you then." He pushed off the locker and stepped away.

"Wait." My voice came out so quiet I was surprised he heard it.

He turned on his heel to face me. "Yeah."

"I don't drive yet. How am I going to get there?" Damn! My tongue had a mind of its own. I wanted to say *no, I'm sorry, I can't.* I knew that was the best choice. There were pros and cons to being the youngest and having three older brothers. They warned me about guys like him. If Mike was here he'd take him apart piece by piece.

He chuckled. "Meet us at Snacktrap. We'll be in a brown Buick." Then he left.

I couldn't get him off my mind all day. There was no kiss, no 'hey babe', nothing like that, yet he wanted me as his girl tonight at the party. *Was he too cool to actually have a girlfriend? Was he embarrassed to call a freshman his girlfriend?* I had so many insecurities and three male brotherly voices shouting in my head.

"Hello! Earth to Emily." Lori's voice drew me from my internal drama.

"Hey."

"So what's going on with Mr. Cool Cobain?" she asked as we walked to the bus.

I shrugged. "I don't know. I don't get him, but I can't say no to him. My mind and tongue aren't connected when he's around. I haven't seen him or heard a word until he shows at my locker today and asks me to go to a party tonight with him."

She rolled her eyes. "So you almost do it with the hottest bad boy in school. What did you expect? His class ring? Oh wait, he doesn't have one."

I caught the low blow to his lack of concern for all things school. "Should I go?"

"Heck yeah, we're going. I wouldn't miss this. We're freshmen. The people there will be upperclassmen. Do you know what this will do for our social status?" Her eyes widened in excitement.

I shuffled my feet in line as we waited for the bus doors to open. "I guess. I hadn't thought of that."

"You're too pure, Em. You really shocked me the other day. I guess there's a wild side to you yet." She pushed a dyed fire-engine-red curl behind her ear.

We devised a plan so our parents wouldn't know what we were really doing. It was pretty cliché. Our parents dropped us at the movie theatre which was in walking distance of the Snacktrap. Lori was always less reserved than me. She had flaming red hair and I wore my natural blond curls. In our relationship I was the blunt object that didn't attempt to break rules, she was the sharp object that lived to break the rules without getting into trouble, yet we got along. I was her conscience and she was the dark angel on my shoulder.

She grabbed my hand and dragged me inside to the restroom. "We need to do something with your face. You can't go to an upperclassmen party with only lip gloss."

She dug mascara, eyeliner, and lipstick from the black skull and crossbones bag she brought everywhere. "Hold still and don't blink," she ordered as she carefully drew black liner beneath and above my eyes. She didn't go heavy, just simple dark lines. Next she rolled the mascara over my lashes then added dark red lipstick.

"Now look," she said.

I turned toward the mirror and barely recognized myself. "You think this is necessary? D was attracted to me without any makeup." I angled my head to check out how different I looked.

"He'll like you more now," was her response.

By the time we got outside a brown Buick was in the parking lot, D resting his back against the front passenger side door. I sucked in a deep breath. He tucked his long, dirty blond hair behind his ears. My pulse quickened.

"I hope you don't mind I brought someone."

"No, she can sit on Delaney's lap. He won't mind." He opened the back door and the front. Lori climbed over the three guys in the back, landing on one of their laps while I scooted into the middle of the front row between Dennis and the driver. He introduced everyone quickly. My heart was beating louder than his voice and I didn't catch their names.

The guys chatted and joked during the drive. Lori remained fairly quiet. She didn't mind taking risks but always calculated them. Despite how she dressed and appeared, she was a straight A student in all Honors classes. I always figured it was her intelligence mingled with being an only child that drove her to compromising circumstances and she always came out untouched and a bit wiser.

We turned off the paved road and drove through the woods until we came to a stop beside other vehicles. They opened the car doors and we climbed out, dispersing in various directions. The area wasn't much of a clearing and there were no houses anywhere nearby that I could see. Plenty of tall trees, students, and alcohol.

"Drinks are in the coolers," D said and walked away, leaving Lori and I.

"That was rude," she stated as she lifted the lid on one of the coolers and sifted through the assortment of alcoholic beverages. She handed me a bottle of orangey liquid and took one for herself.

We drifted through the party and sipped our drinks. I noted she wasn't taking large gulps either which meant she was sizing things up. For me it meant I was unsure, didn't belong with the crowd.

An arm wrapped around my shoulder. "You're sipping soup. Take a swallow," D suggested. His smell lingered in my nose from his proximity.

He pressed his mouth against mine and drove his tongue inside my mouth. Our tongues played a game of chase. Sensations of desire tingled over me until he pulled away and led me further into the woods. I no longer heard the mingle of the partiers, only the distant sound of music.

He wrapped his hand around the bottle of orangey alcohol in mine and lifted it to my lips. "Drink. You need to loosen up."

I was tense, unsure, out of my element, but I followed his direction and took a large gulp. At the time I didn't think about the drink absent from his hand. It was me drinking and within no time I was feeling strange. Not like the other day with the pot but different -- dizzy.

I pushed against his chest. "I don't feel good. I need to sit." I dropped right there. Leaf clutter crunching under my butt.

His hands fondled the top of my head then they left and I heard what sounded like a zipper. I lifted my head to see his cock in his hand.

"Lock those pretty red lips around this."

What? I didn't understand what he was saying. I had no experience with guys. This was far different than holding hands with boys in junior high and small lip pecks. This was the real deal and I didn't know what to do. My inner brother voices all said *Run, Em. This guy is no good.* My body didn't move though. It felt like lead and a little numb.

He rubbed his cock across my face and lifted my chin as he jabbed it at my lips. "Take it in."

Through my quickly fading lucidity, I opened my mouth. His member was firm and soft like velvet. Through the fog in my head he ordered me what to do and I did. My body had no fight. It couldn't move. I blacked out and lost minutes until a creamy, warm, sour liquid coated my throat, waking me. I gagged.

I stared into his face. It was fuzzy at first then swam into clarity. His blue eyes fixed on me. A darkness passed over his irises and suddenly they weren't his eyes but someone else's. A someone; a memory of something. My fuzzy brain snapped to and I drew back and pushed myself onto my feet.

With an unsteady stance I gawked at him. His eyes now his. The menacing ones gone. "I need to go home. I shouldn't be here."

"It's my turn to make you feel good." He grabbed my hands and drew me towards him then pressed his shrunken member against my belly and rubbed. I felt it growing firm.

I pulled away only for him to pull me closer. His hands soon moving down my pants and rubbing my clit. Out of reaction it swelled and became wet. He continued rubbing his cock against me. I lost time again and when I came to my bra and shirt were hiked over my breasts and my legs were in the air one pant leg on, one off. His mouth was caressing my womanhood and circling my entrance.

I moaned as his tongue entered me. That part of me yearning for more, but the sensible part knew it wasn't right. I needed to go. To leave. I pushed up on my elbows and his hand gently pushed against my chest to force me down. His tongue slid from my pussy to my breasts as he lifted himself on top of me. His cock firm and pulsing against my clit as it searched for my entrance.

This was it! He was going to force sex on me. *Was it forcing?* I wanted him. I wanted him so badly, but that wasn't me. It was the part of me that was young and horny. It wasn't right. Sex was meant for someone I loved. A man I'd meet in the future when I was smarter about it. The fog in my mind dissipated in that moment and clarity filled it. Then Mike's voice shouted in my brain *Run, Em!*

His cock finding my entrance, he pushed gently and I pushed against his chest and forced my feet under his legs and with everything I had shoved him off me. I stumbled to my feet and ran. The music and voices became louder. I rested beside a tree to get my bearings and realized I was running with one pant leg off and no shoes. My shirt had dropped into place but my bra was still lifted over my breasts.

As I fixed my clothes I glanced over the crowd searching for Lori. I spotted her and dashed towards her. "It's time to go!" I said and grabbed her arm.

"Sit down, we only just got started," slurred a young man with a ceramic device in his hand shaped and painted like a grim reaper.

Lori's expression faded quick as she took in my appearance. "What happened?"

"We need to go."

She glanced towards the woods where I dashed out of and marched forward. D was there, fully clothed like nothing happened. She stopped in front of him. "How dare you do anything to Em that she didn't want." She brought up her leg and smashed it into his groin quicker then he could back away. Leaving him holding his nuts, she walked away, grabbed my hand, and we left together.

"Wait up," came a female voice.

We stopped. A dark-haired girl ran towards us. She stopped. It was Sierra. "Listen, D is a jerk. I'll take you home."

On the drive home she explained. "I'm really sorry about what he did. If I had known he'd set his sights on you," she glanced at me for a second then shifted her eyes back to the road, "I would have warned you. He does this shit every year!" The anger in her voice resounded in the small cabin of the car.

Lori stayed over that night. The shadows in the corners danced and teased. Small footsteps pounded the hall. I noticed something about them I hadn't in my childhood; they were heavy and the word 'Emily' clung to each step. I glanced at Lori next to me and snuggled closer to her, burying my face beneath the covers.

Chapter 15

Christmas Miracles

The following Monday greeted Lori and me with instant popularity and high fives to Lori as she was the girl who had the guts to kick D in the nuts. It elevated our social status. D never lived it down, nor did he find any more innocent freshmen to bed unwillingly.

All my brothers visited for Christmas that year, which was a gift in itself. Daren was married with two children. His responsibilities to them made it difficult for them to visit more than every couple years. Ray, on the other hand, was too busy being a workaholic bachelor. Mike visited often but hadn't been over since my incident with D. I had no plans on telling him either because he'd crush him to a pulp. As much as I wanted to see that, it wasn't any more right than what D did to me and Lori served him appropriate justice.

It wasn't hard to fool Daren and Ray. They were older and didn't know me like Mike, so the first couple days were easy as they trickled in. I played with my niece and nephew. We brought out old games like *Toss Across* and *Candyland*. I enjoyed them so much I decided then I wanted children. I guess I'd always figured I'd have children. That's what people did when they fell in love and got married but, spending so much time with them, I considered it seriously, deciding I'd have at least two, maybe three.

Mike was the last to make it home. I met him with a hug and tried to stay as cool as possible. I didn't want him to catch onto anything. What happened needed to stay my secret. I wouldn't allow another guy to do that again. It was a hard lesson, but I learned it. My brothers were right, and from now on I'd listen.

We made it through dinner in the town. Our group was so large my father made reservations. We laughed and ate. No problem, everything was normal, and Mike hadn't caught on. Good.

That's what I thought, until that night when Daren and his wife were tucking the children into bed and Ray and my parents were talking. I was sitting up in my bed listening to music, reading a magazine, and Mike snuck in. He didn't knock on the door like a normal person. He came right in and sat on the edge of my bed.

"How are things going?" he asked. His tone gave me a heads up that he was probing.

"High school is different, but I'm getting used to it." Short, simple, my eyes focused on the page in the magazine.

"You're halfway through year one. Each year gets easier. Made any new friends?"

What was he getting at? "Not really. I mostly hang with Lori, sometimes I see Sierra. It's cool knowing a junior."

"Yeah. What about guys? Any boyfriends?" That was it. He hit the hammer on the head of the nail.

That was blunt Mike. He knew something, but I was determined to stay tight-lipped. "Nah. I don't have time. Too much homework."

I hadn't looked at him yet, but focused on the mag in my hands. I wasn't really reading it anymore. I was avoiding eye contact. I felt his eyes staring at my head. I flipped a page. This wasn't me, but if I looked him in the eye the tears behind mine would rush forward and I'd be a slobbering, snotty mess.

"I know you. It's Mike. Tell me what happened." His gentle voice brought the whole incident rushing to my eyes. I squinted them to avoid the assault of tears that wanted to force its way out, followed by my choked words.

He snaked an arm around my neck and lifted his legs onto my bed. He was in for the long haul, anticipating the story. I took in a deep, shaky breath but still didn't look at him. "Nothing happened, Mike." The words came out strangled. That was it. No doubt I was lying and the tears that fell told him that.

"Some guy breaks my sister's heart? You know I'll kill him. A good fist to his face, at least."

I completely broke down then and the words poured from my mouth like a damn flushing toilet. I couldn't make them stop. Safe in his arm and presence was all it took for me to spill everything.

"What's his name?"

"No, Mike. You'll hurt him." A few sobs then I continued. "Lori already kicked him in the nuts. It's over."

"Lori will give me his name."

I gave a shaky sigh. "Fine. It's Dennis. Dennis Cooperton. You happy?"

He nodded. "Where does he live?"

"Mike, don't do anything." I knew he'd find the address, with or without me, so I gave it to him.

"OK, listen, I won't kill him."

We sat on my bed for several quiet minutes, my head resting on his bulky shoulder. He was my Mike. The boyfriend killer from hell. I felt better telling him the story and knowing he would always protect me. Always.

Ray stayed only through Christmas and left the following day. Mike stayed through New Year's but Daren and his family stayed on another few days. They'd gone to dinner and left me with my niece and nephew. I practically fell over volunteering to watch them. The kids were in bed by the time they got back and I was lying in mine, not sleeping, but relaxing to music. Seeing my light on, my mother stepped inside.

"This is the closest thing to being a big sister. How was your night?"

"We watched a movie. They ate mac and cheese and we played games. It was fun. I'm going to miss them." I met her soft, thoughtful gaze.

"Me too. We'll have to visit them again before you graduate and go on to college."

"Mom, that's three and a half years away."

Her lip turned downward. "I know, but the time flies. You're my baby, the last one."

I was the baby. My parents' life would change once I was gone. It would be quieter. They could fill their evenings doing stuff they hadn't since deciding to have children; movies, dinner, adult things.

When I didn't respond she asked, "You want the light off?"

"Sure, I'm getting sleepy." I wasn't overly tired. It had been a busy night and I wanted time to myself.

She flipped it off and left. I tossed and turned trying to get comfortable, then decided to get a drink of milk and a few cookies. As I crept down the hallway I spotted the family room light on and heard two voices, my father and Daren.

"You keep making excuses but that's all they are," Daren said with an upset tone.

"Some things people don't need to know and that's one of them. Aunt Carly even kept her mouth closed." From the tone, I knew my father was upset too.

"One day it may come back and haunt her, you know that?" *Haunt who and what may come back? Was this some deep, dark, buried family secret or were they discussing something else?* All the private conversations I listened to over time made me wonder if there really was a skeleton in the family closet and this one involved Aunt Carly too.

"It's been over five years since he got out and nothing. He was a kid, a mixed up kid, and nobody knows if he was even guilty," my father said in the tone he used to reassure himself. The kind we all use when we make up a lie and want to believe it.

The couch squeaked and Daren spoke. "Who else? The house wasn't broken into. It had to be that twisted fuck."

"I don't care how old you are, watch your mouth in my house!"

"She can handle more than you give her credit for. She's fifteen. What, you think she doesn't see all the crime on the news you watch every night?"

I crept closer until I could see them. Daren sat on the couch and my father stood beside the fireplace with a drink in his hand. "Those people aren't related to her and I don't think fifteen is old enough."

Daren shook his head and threw his hands up. "I guess we'll wait for the sick bastard to find her." He stood abruptly, his eyes boring a hole into my father.

I shot across the hallway into the kitchen but didn't turn the light on until I heard both of them go down the hallway to bed. *Me, they had to be talking about me.* I confirmed this. *Who else?* I was the only fifteen-year-old in their lives.

Nothing in the entire conversation made any sense, and what did Aunt Carly have to do with anything? We'd only seen her once. *Who's the twisted fuck? The sick bastard?* What did the person do and how did it relate to me and Aunt Carly?

I'd never seen her again and assumed she probably died but we never went to her funeral either. Maybe she was just too old and weak to have us around, but I never forgot how I felt around her. There was something about her that was special. Then I remembered how Mike promised to show me pictures of Dad when he was my age. It was a random connection and I still didn't think I looked anything like Dad.

I finished pouring my milk and sat it by the stack of cookies on the bar. In the family room I dug out the photo albums, tossing the ones of me and my brothers into their own pile. I wanted the old ones and found them in the back of the built-in shelves.

One page after the next I turned looking at baby pictures of my father then pictures when he was a bit older and finally when he was a teenager. I stopped a couple times and stared at my grandparents. I'd never met them as they'd died before I was born. His brother too. In the pictures nobody really looked happy. It was sad. I hadn't known my father had lived such a depressing childhood but I was only fitting the emotion I felt into it. Maybe they were really happy but the camera didn't capture it.

He and his brother looked a lot alike and I had to admit I looked a little like both of them, not my hair and eyes but my smile, my cheekbones. At ten, I never would have admitted that, but I was more mature now and saw the unmistakable resemblance. *Was I related to my adoptive father?*

I shuddered. No way! That was preposterous. I pushed closed the album and stuffed them all back the exact way they were, grabbed my cookies and milk, then headed to bed.

As curious as I was, I remembered how we discovered the serial killer who'd been lurking in our neighborhood. It was an adrenaline rush, but also freaky as hell. I agreed with my father, sometimes things were better left secret.

Chapter 16

Bad People and Bad Things

When I went back to school in January, I spotted Dennis. He was the talk of the school. He showed with his arm in a cast and yellowed bruising on his face. The rumor was his pop beat him up. A better guess was my brother got to him.

Judging by the color of his bruises it happened during break. That meant one thing to me -- Mike. I flew through the front door of my house and to my bedroom. I called him again and again until he answered. Not giving him a moment to speak I chewed and yelled his ear off. "I told you not to beat him up, to leave him alone, but you couldn't, could you? No, Mike the *protector* had to take down the boy who tried to rape his sister!" After it came out of my mouth

I realized how crazy my stance was, but either way it wasn't right.

"Hold up! I didn't touch him!" He hollered back so loud I had to move the phone away from my ear.

"I don't believe you. His bruises are yellowed which means it happened sometime during break. You had the motive and could have done it one of those times you went to *Larry's*." I emphasized Larry's because he obviously used his friend as a ruse to pay Dennis the asshole a visit.

"I didn't do it. I mean... I didn't hurt him. He was in one piece when I left."

"So you did go there. I knew it!"

"All I did was put the fucking fear into him. I threatened if he ever hurt another young, innocent girl I'd put my foot so far up his asshole it would come out his mouth."

I chuckled. "You really told him that?"

"Hell yeah! No one hurts my sis."

I relaxed. "Well someone did beat him up, pretty badly. His arm is in a cast and his face is yellow, green, and bluish."

Mike harrumphed. "I'd love to take credit, but it wasn't me. The guy is a real piece of trash. Probably the older brother or father of another girl."

I dropped onto my bed. "I believe you, Mike. It's possible. It could have been."

We talked for a few more minutes then hung up. I was relieved it wasn't Mike, but it made me wonder who did it. *Were the rumors that his father beat the tar out of him true?* I'd been to his house. The mess I saw didn't say much about his pop's housekeeping abilities but that certainly didn't make him an abuser either.

In the hands of nosey teens, by the next day in school the story had grown in leaps and bounds. His father also disappeared, which wasn't entirely odd since, according to kids who knew him, his father took off all the time. Dennis never knew if it was work -- his father was a truck driver --

or if he was running around with women. Evidently the apple didn't fall far from the tree. I hadn't known any of this about Dennis and was a bit shocked. I had never seen him as a victim, only myself.

It was a few days later when all hell broke loose. Dennis was in school that day. Several police showed which got the attention of the drama-fueled, hormonal student body. Rumors spread like a forest fire when they took Dennis out of school.

His father's body was found floating face-up in the river that ran through town. It grossed me out a lot since that same river flowed through the woods at the edge of my subdivision. He could have floated by my house. A man and his boy out for a day of fishing found him.

It wasn't that crime didn't happen but the only time I'd been this close to it was the mystery we solved when I was ten. Dennis never came back to school. It was rumored he killed his father and was sent to juvenile prison. I didn't know if that was the truth. The only part of the

story that made the paper or the news
was the man and his son finding
Dennis' pop floating face-up.

Chapter 17

Sweet First Love

By the time I was a junior, I made the Varsity Cheer Squad. Lori was in all AP classes and headed toward possible valedictorian. I met my first real boyfriend. He was kind, gentle, and a foreign exchange student from Spain -- Augustin. He was a year ahead of me.

It was never meant to last, but I gave him myself willingly and lovingly. That night was my template for love with a man. We planned it. The day after his graduation he took me to dinner. The candle light shone in his dark eyes as we feasted on lobster.

In the room, I gave myself to him willingly as his hands caressed me and our lips met in a passionate kiss. I enveloped myself in the moment, soaking in each touch to my body that sent shivers of pleasure coursing through me. His hands so gentle and soft. His lips candy on mine.

"I love you, Emily," he whispered breathlessly as his lips lulled me into submission.

"I love you, Augustin." I meant it. He was my first love and I never forgot him.

He slid his member inside me, slowly, carefully. "Tell me, please, if it hurts."

It was so large and stung in a good way, a way I wanted. I cringed in pleasure and pain as he worked his way inside me. "Oh."

He stopped and lifted his head. "I'm sorry. I will stop."

"No, keep going," I assured him.

His brows lowered. "Are you sure?"

I nodded, then drew my lips to his, whispering, "Yes."

After the pinch, the pain subsided and he slid in and out, swelling more and more until he was breathless and holding me firm as he shuddered.

Rolling to the side he held an arm over my chest. It was a moment I tried to capture but, as moments do, eventually they fade. "You feel so good. Thank you."

His politeness was something from his culture. He grew up using his manners unlike most American boys. After D, I hadn't trusted or dated many and was always turned off by what they expected. Augustin didn't expect. He was grateful and generous. "I'm going to miss you."

That's why we were here. He was leaving in a couple days to return to his college studies in Spain. We'd talk and write, even email, but eventually we'd grow apart. He'd meet a nice Spanish woman and I'd meet a nice American man, if there was one to be found.

He rubbed the curls from my forehead. "I will miss you, Emily." His lips met mine in a passionate kiss.

I cried for three days after he left. My inner teenager wasn't as mature as it thought it was. The idea I'd never see him again set in with crushing pain.

Lori stole me away to Nags Head. She said it was our last chance to do something like this together. Next year we'd be seniors and after that heading to college and starting new lives. We stayed in a cheap motel straddled with age cracks in the cement and big pink flower bedspreads. The air blew too cold but the sun over the beach and warmth on my skin put me at peace.

We did what kids with no adult supervision do: partied. I did with skepticism, remembering all too clearly what happened with D. Lori did with abandon. By the time we made it home our skin was dark brown, our minds a bit wiser, and our bond tighter than ever before. It's what happened next in my life that tossed it in a tizzy.

Chapter 18

Anamnesis

My parents never spoke about Aunt Carly. From time to time, Mike and I did, recalling fondly the month we spent with her. When I came home one afternoon from spending the day with Lori and met my parents with narrowed eyes and creased foreheads, I knew something serious had happened. It was what came out of their mouths that shocked me.

Dad sat on the couch, his hands folded on his knees as he leaned forward and met my gaze. "Aunt Carly passed away yesterday."

I had thought of her often but, since we hadn't seen her, considered she'd already passed on to greater things. If she'd been alive all this time, why hadn't we spent another summer with her? *Why hadn't she visited for the holidays?* I was almost more upset that she'd been alive all this time. "What?"

"She passed away in her sleep last night from natural causes. Your mom and I will be attending the funeral--"

I cut him off midsentence. "I'm going too. You never even knew her. Mike and I did. So I'm going, and paying my respects." I stood, ready to storm from the room.

My father opened his mouth to speak but my mother's gentle, rational words came out first. "Of course." She glanced at my father.

He sighed heavily and nearly choked on his words. "Of course."

"I'll go pack!" I stomped from the room as if I was in charge. Once I made it into the hallway I slowed my pace and listened. Over the years of eavesdropping I'd learned they had a knack for private talk about me far more than any of my brothers.

It was odd really. I wasn't their blood child. They adopted me so long ago I couldn't remember a life without them. I'd never felt anything less than their child, yet they had many whispered conversations about me.

The following day we arrived at Aunt Carly's house. It looked the same, but wasn't. Her absence made it feel like an old, lonely house. I went room to room while my parents sat down with the lawyer who let us inside.

Every room, I expected to find her, but didn't. The weight of reality crashed in on me and tears ran over my cheeks, dropping onto my shirt. I pushed aside her clothes in the closet and stared at the basement door, remembering with clarity the day Mike and I found it. We were curious kids. She should have been angry with us, yelled at us, or at the least scolded us, but she didn't. Instead she told us the secrets of her past.

I pushed the door open and stared into the dark abyss, then flipped the switch and watched the lights turn on like falling dominoes. One step in, I halted when I heard my mother's voice. Not wanting her to know of this super-secret part of Aunt Carly's life I turned the lights off and stepped back, closing the door and returning the clothes to their rightful spots.

"What are you doing in here?" my mother asked from a few feet away.

"The house is lonely without her."

My mom's arms wrapped around my shoulders. "I know."

How could she know? She barely knew her. I let it slide as the warmth and love of my mother's embrace dried the tears as I cried into her shoulder.

I awoke in the early hours, just before the sun rose, to the scent of freesia. "Aunt Carly." I pushed upwards in bed and studied the room. Dim light filtered through the windows causing the dark shadows in the corners to depart. It was dumb, of course, because she was dead. There was no possible way she could be in my room, yet I smelled her presence.

I inhaled the freesia and sank back into sleep, waking about nine and slipping downstairs. Caren had breakfast waiting; fresh fruit, croissants, and quiche. The sound of Daren's voice caught me off guard.

"How are you doing, Em?" He filled a mug of coffee then took a seat beside me.

"When did you get here?" I really wanted to ask why. As far as I knew, he'd never met Aunt Carly. He was an accountant, not a lawyer, and where was his family? On second thought, a funeral wasn't an appropriate place for two small children.

He took a sip of coffee, his face wrinkling from the heat. "About an hour ago."

By mid afternoon the house was filled with people, none that I knew with the exception of my family, Caren and Jessie -- Aunt Carly's servants.

Her body was cremated. The urn with her ashes on a table. A colorful assortment of flowers surrounded it. It was a celebration of her life. I overheard conversations as I milled about the room.

"You must be Carly's great niece," said an unfamiliar voice.

I lifted my eyes from the table with Aunt Carly's ashes. Deep wrinkles were embedded in the woman's light skin and a crown of gray was styled on her head. "Yes."

"You have her eyes and hair. She was always beautiful but in her youth her looks turned many heads."

"I..." I paused there, considering my words. This wasn't the time to tell her we weren't blood related. It was a commemoration of her life. "Thank you." I smiled.

"You be careful with those young men." She winked. "Choose one that deserves you."

She continued past, leaving me confused. The moment was strange and left an unsettling feeling in my gut.

The following morning, I woke early before anyone else in the house, drifted downstairs. Gently cupping the urn in my hands, I carried her ashes outside and down the trail. The lake is where she'd want to spend eternity with the fond memories of her husband.

The trail was wet with dew and the bench deserted without her. I stared at the still water. Tall, bushy trees were mirrored there. I sucked in a deep breath. I'd get heat from my parents for this but my instincts said it was the right thing to do. The thing she'd wanted done.

I lifted the lid from the urn and stared into the ashes. It was difficult to believe she was inside this. Tears rolled over my cheek as I walked along the water's edge, spreading her ashes over the water. They glistened and dissolved.

I took her spot on the bench, absorbing her presence, and swore I felt her warmth and a breeze carrying freesia.

"Emily?" asked my brother Daren, breaking the peaceful moment I shared with my dead aunt.

I turned. His eyes were fixed on the urn beside me.

"You didn't?"

I nodded. "I did. It's what she'd have wanted."

"Those ashes weren't yours."

"No, they were hers. She liked this spot because it reminded her of the time she and her late husband spent here," I said defensively.

"What makes you think that?"

I bit back, "You wouldn't know because *you* didn't know her. *I did*. We connected."

My brother surprised me when he joined me on the bench. "Emily, there are somethings you should know." An unmistakable uncertainty in his voice.

I made eye contact with him. His eyes studied me as I studied him. "There are things Mom and Dad keep from you, but I think it's wrong. You need to know."

I overheard the many whispered conversations. They didn't keep things from me, only thought they did, but all the little secrets I didn't want to know. A tiny part of me did, but I always shut it down. My gaze still locked on his, I stayed silent, allowing him to speak. The tiny part of me that wanted answers was present.

"It's because of Aunt Carly that Mom and Dad found you and they should have told you this a long, long time ago. Aunt Carly found you first in the paper. Your family didn't die in a car wreck but a home invasion. It made the headlines."

Home invasion. I tried hard to remember why that sounded familiar, as if somehow I'd known that or heard it before. It wasn't my family, but someone else's. I just couldn't place whose, or maybe it was something I heard on TV.

A slight breeze blew a blond ringlet over my cheek. He smoothed it behind my ear. "Mom and Dad really wanted a little girl, especially Mom. They were so excited."

I butted in, "Aunt Carly wanted a little girl too -- her niece -- but the state wouldn't let her adopt and..." I grew quiet. I got it. When she saw the story of my family she wanted me but was too old by that time so she found my parents.

Daren's nod confirmed my thoughts. "How do you know that?"

"Mike and I found stuff in the basement. We were snooping and shouldn't have been." I sighed. "That's when she found us and told us the story. How her niece's father, her brother, went to jail for the bad things he'd done and his wife committed suicide. The girl was a teenager by then and at first didn't want anything to do with Aunt Carly, but then she did after she got married and then they died..." The words hung in the air, lengthening the distance between us.

Died; they died. It was something about their death that I should remember. It lengthened in the air then left with the gentle breeze that threatened to loosen the strand of hair Daren had pushed behind my ear.

I promised Aunt Carly I'd never tell, but now, with her passed on, I guessed I wasn't hurting anything. If she was a random woman she really had no connection to our family. "So she's not really Mom's aunt and has no blood relation to the family?"

"No, she's not related to Mom and Dad."

"Why me? I get she wanted a girl and all but I'm not special or kin. Nothing. Why?"

His brows creased. "Think about it. You know this, Em."

I didn't get it. It didn't make sense. People die all the time. Why would the story of one family and one little girl make someone find that little girl a family and why would she choose my parents out of the hundreds of thousands of people she could have chosen?

Daren noted the question mark on my face as if he was reading my mind. "Aunt Carly was a very wealthy woman. She spared no expense paying for our college, buying the house you live in. Why would someone do that?"

Love. That was the only thing that made sense, but how could this woman love me? *Why would she love me? She's my aunt.*

His expectant expression turned to relief. That was it. He recognized my wide mouth and eyes. There was no need to say the words.

She was truly my aunt and that's why I looked so much like her. A sinister thought sat off the coast of my brain, in a dark place I couldn't reach.

The conversation left my mind spinning. My parents were murdered. That was the ugly word and I was alive. It didn't change that dead was dead and I didn't care to know more. Darkness didn't have a place in my world.

The hair on my arms stood at attention, my gut twisted into a knot like a tight ball of string, and shadows crept from the corners of my mind, shaping into blurry figures. I forced it back, not yet ready to face whatever it was.

My willful ignorance and gut-wrenching fear of my past is what put me in the position I'm in now. My mind riding the waves of my life in search of the answers.

Chapter 19

Dust of the Past

I took a pass that evening when my family went out for dinner. Once the car was through the gates I pulled the attic steps down. Mike and I had found pictures and it was due to my conversation with Daren that I now needed to see the evidence that Carly was kin to me.

I pulled the string, lighting the attic. Shadows played in the corners as I drifted closer to the boxes with the photo albums. Dust tickled my nose and I sneezed, cutting through the deathly silence that sent shivers rippling over my body. It wasn't this creepy when Mike was with me.

A creak followed each of my steps as I slowly moved toward the albums, my eyes darting from corner to corner. It felt like several breathless minutes had passed when I finally made it to the albums, spilled as we'd left them. No one had been in the attic since Mike and me.

I picked up the one lying on the floor. The one I'd dropped while fleeing the room so many years ago. I opened the book and flipped to the picture of the little blond girl. I hadn't noted before her solemn face. She lacked a smile. I stared into her blue eyes, yellowed with age. They were but mere windows into a forlorn soul.

I set the album back in the box where it belonged, the home I'd taken it from, and turned to leave. In that instant water rained down on the house, echoing through the attic. My foot slid on something, causing me to lose my balance. I dropped backwards, catching myself with my hands. A slip of paper shot from beneath my foot.

I leaned forward and grabbed it. The lights flickered then cut off before I could get a look at the faces. The pitter patter of rain played on the roof as if trying to give me a message. It turned into small, heavy footsteps. Moonlight drifted through the windows and the shadows in the corners moved towards me. Boxes became a fuzzy face and the footsteps grew louder as if they were moving towards me.

My breath caught and my heart did summersaults as I crawled with the pictures in hand towards the steps. *Thump, thump, thump.* My ears couldn't discern the difference between the steps and my heartbeat. Once down the steps, I folded the ladder and let it snap into place with a loud bang and ran to my room, slamming the door into place and pushing a chair in front of it.

I dropped the pictures onto my dresser and buried myself under the covers, tightening into a ball. Each beat of my heart thumping in my ears.

The footsteps stopped with the rain and car doors closed. *They were home!* I threw the covers off me and scooted the chair away from the door, using moonlight to scramble down the steps. My heartbeat returned to normal when I saw their faces. I wanted to jump into my father's arms for the safety they provided me as a child.

My mom lit candles in the living room and we played cards with the light it provided until our yawns became contagious. I set a candle on the dresser beside the bed. Light spread in a circle and flickered on the ceiling and walls, lulling me to sleep.

In the morning I packed my things, then remembered the pictures. The objects I wanted enough to climb into the attic to find. A place filled with unwanted memories. I flipped them over and stared again at the little girl. Moving that picture below the other, I stared at the faces of three children. Their eyes as hollow and as devastated as the blond girl, except for the largest boy. His stared into my soul. I wondered for a moment what he saw. When a dark film appeared to coat the blue of his eyes I dropped the picture as if it was glass that cut my hand. Then I remembered that's what happened the last time I looked at the picture -- as if his eyes were alive inside the two-dimensional picture.

I blew out a breath, picking the picture up again, and ripped around the older boy then brought him to the flame still flickering on the candle. The edges turned black and ate a circle around his face and twisted it into a misshapen mess. Blackened holes ate his cheeks, working their way to his dark-shadowed eyes until they enveloped him.

The heat of the flame suddenly burnt my finger and I dropped the ashes left of him on the candle holder and stepped away. I studied the faces of the other children. A small boy and little girl, her blond ringlets familiar, and deep blue sorrowful eyes. I knew her from somewhere. At that time my mind was not ready to accept who she was. I compared them to the little blond girl and noted the resemblances. They were related, had to be.

I stared into the mirror. I held the pictures, one to each side of my face, and studied them. Curls stuck out like needles from my head like the girls', only theirs were brushed. The little girls' eyes were almost the same, as if they could be the same child reincarnated. The one in the picture with the boy had the same shade of blue as mine. The other picture was too old to tell, but I guessed she also had the same shade before the picture yellowed.

I swallowed hard. Glimmers of recognition, blurs of the past, threatened to surface. I shuddered and placed the pictures face-down on the dresser then shuffled them into my hand and dropped them into the pocket of my suitcase.

Lori sat cross-legged on my bed across from me. I spread out the pictures. Her eyes went straight to the one I'd torn the hideous little boy out of. "What happened to this and who's in that picture with you? It's not Mike."

"That's not me. I don't know who he is or who she is."

"You found these at your aunt's house and she's really your aunt. Maybe you have a twin?"

I hadn't thought of that. Anything was possible. I'd already told her about my conversation with Daren. It rattled me off my kilter and was impossible to keep inside. As my best friend she knew as much about me as I did. "I guess, but if I had a twin she's dead. My entire birth family is dead."

She shrugged. "I think it's you. I've known you most of your life and this picture looks like you."

I blew out a breath and thrust the other picture at her. "What about this girl?"

"She looks a lot like this girl. They're probably relatives of yours. Maybe you should research this and find out more about your birth family." Her words sliced into my chest like a sword as they casually rolled off her tongue.

"They're dead. There's nothing to know." I tightened my arms over my folded legs.

"You're so tense. Daren seems to know a lot, ask him."

I shook my head.

"You have this way of facing fear head-on rather than shrinking back as if a tiger is getting ready to swat your face. Your past is only a mystery because you let it be. You showed me these wanting answers and now you're shrinking back, running from an unknown darkness that only exists because you let it. Knowledge is power."

I grabbed the pictures and shuffled them, placing the ripped one on the bottom.

"Emily, you're scared. I get it."

I dropped my legs off the bed and stood. "No, you don't. You have two parents who gave birth to you. My family is all I have and I'm their daughter, even if not biologically. I don't need this family." I tossed the pictures into the waste can beside my desk.

A smile tugged at Lori's lips. "I pushed a button! Go on, let it out."

There was nothing more to say. Aunt Carly was dead and any skeletons in my blood family's past went with her. "What did you get on your ACTs?"

"So that's how you're going to play this. Ignore it. That's exactly what I'm talking about, Emily." She sighed and noted my "I'm done" expression. "Fine, I got a thirty-one."

It was her words that helped me realize my strength came when Mike was present. His presence made me feel indestructible and courageous. On my own, I hid under the covers.

Chapter 20

Prince Charming

A year later we were in college, looking forward to our first summer break. I'd only seen Lori at Christmas, even though we spoke often. She was busy making straight As and I was busy getting into a sorority. That's how I met Eric.

It was a party between the frat he was pledging and the sorority I was pledging. His eyes locked onto mine from across the room and the world stood still for that moment. We spent the evening talking, sipping on drinks, then escaped together. College social life suddenly felt small compared to the intense feeling I had for him. It was unexplainable. Love at first sight. All I knew was, at that moment and for the rest of college, it's all that mattered aside from getting my degree.

As a freshman, I had no choice but to board in the same sex dorms with two other roommates. Our schedules were so different we barely saw each other and I spent most of my time in the common areas with Eric.

It was the time between afternoon and evening, the sun sinking below the horizon. Brilliant shades of red spread over the sky. I walked into the local mom and pop grocery located outside the campus. The college students often went there because everything was cheaper than on campus. We probably kept the store open.

The white brick front was friendly and clean. The bold green sign was welcoming. The couple who ran it, always smiling. They kept everything we needed from tampons to alcohol to crackers and cheese. The bell hanging from the door ding-donged as I strolled in.

Mr. Cole, the store owner, glanced upward from his books, lowered his glasses and said, "Good evening, Emily." They knew us all by name.

"Good evening," I responded. He went back to his books and I strolled the store, filling the basket I grabbed. I tossed in a few microwave pizzas and grabbed a couple small bottles of juice than perused the beauty aisle.

A man leaned over a box, grabbed bottles, and placed them on the shelves. He was directly in my way. "Excuse me, I need a bottle of *Fine Botanicals* shampoo for curly hair."

The man grabbed the bottle, turned, and handed it to me. My breath caught and the basket in my hands dropped to the floor with a crash.

"Emily?"

I couldn't speak. My words fled and my feet were frozen to the ground. Before me stood D, his hair short above his ears like a military cut.

"Everything OK?" asked Mr. Cole as he came around the aisle. "I heard the crash."

I swallowed hard, searching for my voice. I only got as far as opening my mouth.

"This young lady dropped her basket is all," D answered as he leaned over, placing all my items into the basket.

Mr. Cole's eyes searched mine as I stood stock still like a mannequin. "I see you've met Dennis. He's been a big help."

My eyes pleaded for Mr. Cole to read my mind as I grabbed the basket from D's hand and edged towards Mr. Cole. "I'm ready to check out." I let out a deep breath. Being further away from D, my voice returned. I nearly ran to the checkout counter.

Mr. Cole's brows straightened like a thin pencil below his wrinkled forehead. "Is everything OK, Emily?"

I nodded. "Yes, fine." The air in the store felt stuffy and my knees wobbled. I blinked several times to keep my vision straight.

He eyed me as he rang the items. "Seven thirty-one."

I tossed him a ten and took a deep breath. I didn't look behind me and ran back to campus. Instead of going to my lonely room I went to

Eric's building. He met me in the lounge.

"Emily, look at me. What happened?" He wrapped his hands around my arms and stared deep into my eyes, searching for the answer. The green of his irises and his hands on my skin eased my worried soul.

I swallowed and, before the words made it out, I was pressed against his firm chest, crying onto his shoulder. He held me tight, dropping kisses onto my head. After a couple minutes he snuck me upstairs to his room.

My tears dried and the story of D rolled out of my mouth. I'd only known Eric for a month but it felt like an eternity. We were connected, making it feel safe to tell him the most horrifying experience of my life.

"I'm so sorry, Emily." He brought my head to his chest and combed his hands through my hair. Next our lips were locked and our tongues found each other. The dreadful experience with D sank back to the shadowy corners of my mind and I gave myself to Eric.

His soft caresses over my nipples sent ripples of pleasure over my entire body. I wanted to devour him as I pulled his shirt over his head and dropped it to the floor. Soon, all our clothes littered the area around his bed. Our bodies pressed together. His hard member searching for my pleasure spot as it worked its way inside me. A small gasp left my lips. I hadn't had sex since Augustin.

My hands roved his back, my lips kissed his neck and ears. He lifted up, kissing my breasts, sending pleasure to my pussy. I moaned in desire. I wanted more of him, all of him. He slid in and out, met by each thrust of my hips until we were panting. Our craving for each other sufficed for the moment as orgasms wracked our bodies.

I lay with my head on his chest, my hand twisting the few dark hairs there. I loved that he wasn't furry like a gorilla. Being near a trusted man was a strength for me. I'd gone to Eric seeking safety like I felt with my brothers. It gave me courage, made me feel like I could face

anything in life so long as I had Eric
or one of my brothers beside me.

Chapter 21

A Pack of Wolves

By summer we found an apartment together. My parents paid for my share. Really, Aunt Carly's money paid for it. I hadn't told my family I was living with a man. They hadn't even met Eric yet. With three brothers, one an overprotective Mike, I figured it was better this way. It was Thanksgiving before they met him.

I sighed relief when they seemed to accept him, even Mike. It didn't happen right away. Mike warmed up to him after spending a day with him. My heart pounded in my chest and I imagined all sorts of stuff that could happen with Mike and Eric alone. He'd taken him fishing and they'd left early in the morning.

Fishing only seemed like an innocent activity but out in the woods alone Mike could drown him, beat the tar out of him, push him in the way of a wild animal like a black bear, a coyote or a pack of wolves that would devour his body leaving only a set of bones. I plastered myself to a book but it didn't help take my mind off the horrors that Eric might face alongside my protective and buff older brother.

When they came home, in one piece and laughing, the blood in my veins settled and my heartbeat returned to normal. We returned home the day before our classes started back up to unpack and clean our laundry. Eric's laundry. I'd taken mine with me but he refused to bring his even though I assured him it was fine.

He declined any assistance and even took on a part time job to make extra money. His scholarship covered classes, books, and even part of his board, but any extras came out of his pocket. Living off-campus we had more expenses. He was proud and spent his life working for what he had. Everything I had was given to me; even the new car that sat in the parking lot below our apartment. Our lives were night and day, yet our love for each other was intense.

It was my trust in him that brought about what happened next. We were discussing my family and he brought up how much I looked like my father. "You get the same expression when you're irritated. The one where you clamp your mouth tight and your eyes become slits. He did the same thing when Mike said 'We're going fishing tomorrow'. I saw the wheels spinning in your father's head. I wasn't worried. I'm an older brother too. I'd do anything for my little sister."

I sucked in my bottom lip. "I have to tell you something."

His eyes took on an intense green, as they did when he was serious. I shifted my mouth. This shouldn't be a hard thing to say but the tenseness of my muscles said the opposite. "Eric. I'm adopted."

"Hmm... in psychology I learned that a person can take on characteristics of those they spend a lot of time with. Probably why you look so much like your family."

"I do?" The father stuff I'd heard before and I admitted to myself we looked a bit alike, but what was this family thing?

He nodded. "Yeah, your dad and your brothers. Definite resemblances in expressions and mannerisms."

I stood then and dug the pictures of the little blond girls from the special place I kept them and placed them on the table in front of him. "What about these?"

He studied them. "What happened to this one?" He pointed to the ripped picture.

"It doesn't matter. Do I look like them?"

"These aren't you?"

I punched his shoulder gently and rolled my eyes. "No. I wouldn't ask if they were."

"Ouch." He rubbed his arm as if the punch really hurt. "I mean, really, this one especially and the boy in it too. They look like you. I mean lots younger but their heart-shaped faces, blond ringlets. And check out the little girl; see how that one curl over her forehead springs in the opposite direction of the others. Yours does that. When you wake up. It's adorable." He gently pulled a ringlet and twisted it in his finger. "This one right here."

I'd never noticed that. I'd stared at the pictures so many times over the years. This was my connection to the biological family I didn't know. "They aren't me, but are relatives. I never met them." I spilled the entire story about my Aunt Carly and how Mike and I found the pictures and how I went up in the attic years later and stole them.

"What was your name before you were adopted?"

I lowered my brows. "Emily. My name's always been Emily."

His lips curled in an awkward smile. "Your last name."

I shrugged.

"Don't you have your birth certificate? You've never looked at it?"

"My parents have it. I've never even seen it, but it doesn't matter. My family is my family and, to be honest,"

I paused for a second preparing to reveal my deepest fear, "I think there's something sinister about my biological family. I can't explain it but--" I let the words hang. "They died, were murdered."

His Adam's apple bobbed, revealing a hard swallow and he licked his lips before forming the next words. "I get that, Emily. Why you feel like that about them. I told you my father died, but not how. He was killed senselessly when he went to the local gas station to fill up and get my mom a gallon of milk for her pregnancy cravings with my sister. Chocolate milk. She drank it like it was going out of style."

My heart dropped. I knew the next words before he said them.

"He was killed when the station was held up. A gallon of milk, a tank of gas, and a bullet to his brain."

I grabbed him and pulled him to me. "I'm so sorry." Tears dropped like a thunderstorm, carving rivers over my cheeks. It wasn't only his loss, but that we had the same type of loss. Unforgiving losses due to the violence of another, at the hands of someone that could take a life and not shed a tear for their families or their precious lives. And the small whisper in the dark shadows of my brain that the little girl was me, the boy my brother and the little girl in the yellowed picture my mother.

"It's OK, Emily. I was eleven. It's been a long time and my mom worked her ass off to take care of us, often working two jobs."

I held him tighter. That's why he was so proud and stubborn. He'd learned hard work pays the bills and cares for the family. I hadn't understood that until that moment as the epiphany struck hard. "I love you, Eric Turnwell." I pressed my lips to his.

Chapter 22

A Well of Gold

We married soon after graduation. I was six weeks pregnant, but I never told anyone except Eric. We didn't keep any secrets from each other. A week later we returned from our honeymoon. A trip my parents paid for. Eric hadn't been happy about it, too proud to accept a cruise to Bermuda as a wedding gift, but gave in when he saw how excited I was and how much I wanted it. This would be our chance to spend time together before parenthood.

It was the day after we returned that I got the phone call from a lawyer, Mrs. McCuffy. A large chunk of Aunt Carly's estate went to me. There was no explanation why, but I knew. I was her biological grandniece. Possibly the only blood family left to inherit her huge fortune. Most people would be ecstatic to learn they were millionaires overnight, but not Eric. It was our first argument and ended our honeymoon bliss.

His brows drawn into a V, he laid a fist on the table. "No, Emily! No, we aren't taking the money, not when so many other people are struggling in life."

Changing his mind was like moving a sturdy column. "Eric, it's not your choice. The money is mine and we could use it at least some of it. We can also donate to charity. There's plenty to go around. She wanted this for me and was possibly the only biological family I had left in this world." Tears threatened to erupt as I sucked back the growing wetness in my nose.

He stamped out of the room without a word, the front door slamming behind him. The monster tears dropped from my eyes and I cupped my face into my hands. *What was wrong with money?*

When the tears dried and I caught my breath again, I sifted around the apartment tidying things, dusting, fluffing, and anything to settle my mind. Eric never had what I did. He didn't have a rich aunt. I thought I understood that, but I didn't. Selfishly, I wanted to keep all the money. We'd never want for anything ever, but he was right the money could be used for more than our desires. There were people who didn't have and needed. Hard working people like his mom. She was a gentle, kind soul, who often worked two jobs to care for her children.

The front door creaked open and footfalls moved toward the kitchen where I sat drinking an herbal tea.

"Emily." He took the seat next to me and placed my hands in his. "Don't say anything. I know what it's like to struggle and to lose a parent violently, but I don't know what it's like to be adopted and not have a biological family. We should keep some of the money. It can get us started with a house and you wouldn't have to work when the baby is born. We could also put some in trust for our children so they can go to college, but I think the rest should go to hard working people who struggle like my mom and live payday to payday."

I wrapped my arms around Eric's neck. My perfect man who wasn't without flaws. The alligator tears flowed again. "I couldn't agree with you more."

He folded his arms around me. We settled our first marital uprising.

Seven months later, our first son was born -- Ethan Turnwell. Over the next several years, we had our ups and downs but always settled things diplomatically and had another son, then I got pregnant again. That's when all the fractured memories of my life began joining together; only I didn't make the connection. The horror lay on the precipice of conscious thought but never went over the line.

Chapter 23

Rhythm of the Heart

The fake leather of the table cold on my butt, a paper shirt and gown drawn over the top of my not-yet-swollen belly. A knock on the door alerted me the doctor was coming in.

"How are you today?" she asked with a warm smile.

"Doing good."

"And how's the baby?" She leaned back against the counter.

"Everything seems normal."

"That's good." She nodded her head and pushed off the counter.

Going through the usual motions, she measured my belly, jotted down notes, assured me I was the right size for the length of my pregnancy. She then depressed the stethoscope and listened. Her eyes squared and wrinkles became prominent on her forehead. She moved the stethoscope around, her expression unchanged.

"You want to listen?" she asked.

Of course! What mother wouldn't? She handed me the earpiece which I placed in my ears. As she slid the stethoscope over my belly I heard something I hadn't with the boys, an echo. "What is that?"

She sighed. "Well it may be nothing at all, sometimes the position of the baby makes an echo or it could be twins."

My jaw dropped. "Twins?"

She nodded. "Usually twins run in the family, anyone else have twins?"

I shook my head. I didn't know anything about them. Aunt Carly didn't have children but she was a triplet. "Wait, my aunt, she was a triplet."

"We can't be sure yet. I'm ordering an ultrasound which should confirm whether or not there are two babies in there or just one." She handed me a doctor's scribed note on letterhead paper.

I didn't know whether to be excited or frightened. Twins? I'd never considered the possibility. It would mean two of everything and a strain on our budget. I took in a deep breath as I pulled the car into the garage. If I was having twins, so be it. We'd find a way to make it work.

Eric pushed the door open five twenty-three on the dot. The boys ran towards him. They each grabbed a leg. He took each step as if they were heavy as weights. "I can't mo…ve. You got me!" He dropped onto the couch and the boys giggled. It was a daily game they played.

I leaned my arm against the entryway between the living room and kitchen. I wasn't sure how he would take the possible twin news so I'd made his favorite Italian chicken with tons of mozzarella, loaded garlic-cheese bread and salad.

After a few minutes the boys ran off, bounding through the hallway into their room. Eric stood and took me in his arms. "The house smells as delicious as you taste." He grabbed my ass as his lips pressed against mine.

"You taste pretty good yourself." I rubbed my hand against his cock.

"Mmm... stop or I'll take you here," he joked.

"We can push everything off the counter, get a quickie in before the boys are back," I teased.

"So tempting." He gave my ass one more squeeze then backed away. "What's the occasion?"

I licked my lips. "Does there need to be one?"

"Not at all, but the look on your face tells me there is."

I could never keep anything from him. Not for a second. "I went to the doctors today."

His brows dropped into a V. "And? Everything OK?"

"Would I be making your favorite if something was wrong?"

He shrugged. "Absolutely not. So what's the news?"

This was the moment of reckoning. I sucked in a deep breath

and spit out the words. "We might be having twins."

He sat up straight. "Twins?"

I nodded with an anxious smile on my face.

His face lit up. "That's great! I mean, it'll be tough, but its wonderful news. Maybe we'll have two girls to bring out the soft side in those two rough and tumble boys."

His elation made my spirits high. It wasn't that I expected anger but something else. The news of possible twins was huge, however, he smiled the rest of the day as if it was the best news ever.

Two nights later, cramping woke me from a dead sleep. I crumpled in pain, holding my belly. "Eric." The word tense and breathless. The baby, or babies, something was wrong. I shouldn't be having period cramps.

The sound of my labored words woke him with a start. He jolted up and stared wide-eyed at me. "Emily? What is it?" He noted my hands on my belly. "The babies?"

I nodded then he pulled back the covers to jump out of bed and the sheet was soaked in crimson. I screamed.

"I got this, honey. Lay down."

He grabbed the cell he kept on the night stand and called Mrs. Meelan -- an older woman who lived across the street. She was a sweet lady who we often talked with and had watched the boys a few times when we snuck in dates.

Within a few minutes she was at the door and Eric was carrying me to the car. The bleeding seemed to have stopped, but the cramps hadn't. My nerves a jumble, the whole event is fuzzy. The hospital, the doctor, everything until they rolled in the ultrasound machine.

"The baby's heartbeat is strong but an ultrasound will tell us more," the doctor said as the tech took a seat in a rolling chair and squeezed a glop of cold jelly on my belly.

"Uh huh," the tech murmured. Then after what felt like several breathless minutes said, "Everything looks A OK. The baby is the right size, development is completely normal." He turned the screen so we could see everything and pointed out the baby's head, heart that pounded steady, the baby's tiny abdomen.

"The baby?" Eric asked.

The tech nodded. "Were you expecting something else?" he joked.

"No, the baby is perfect."

At twelve weeks, it was too soon to determine the sex and a copy of the ultrasound report would go to my doctor.

The doctor filled in the gaps. "It's not uncommon to have bleeding and sometimes that comes with cramping. You did the right thing in coming here. As you can see, the baby is healthy. Make an appointment with your regular obstetrician."

I swallowed. "What could cause that?"

He folded his hands and glanced from me to Eric. "Many things. We will run a few more tests but I think you and the baby are fine - - just a scare."

Before we left, the nurse handed me a booklet that contained all sorts of problems during pregnancy. She explained each one. It was morbid, but our baby was fine and healthy. I was even a bit relieved that I wasn't having twins because that would mean two butts to change and my breasts would never get a rest. I'd be a milking diaper-changer. Hours ago I was readying my mind for that, now I was so happy there was a single baby.

Guilt ate at me for the next few weeks for even allowing myself the happiness of a single baby birth. Those feelings were cut short when something more sinister happened.

Chapter 24

Cometh the Stalker

Eric took the day off and came with me to the ultrasound appointment. He was as excited as me and when they said it was a girl a grin took over his face. We watched our daughter move inside me. Her tiny hands and feet developed. She was perfect.

The grin on Eric's face stayed as we ate lunch. The staff bustled around us and chatter filled the restaurant but the grin was immovable. "We should name her Erin."

Since we both had E names we stuck to the theme with our children. "Erin. I like it." I rubbed my belly. "Erin you are."

His green eyes glowed and twinkled. In his world, at that moment, was only us.

We picked the boys up from school. Brooding clouds covered the sky. Eric pulled the car into the garage only moments before the storm hit. When the rain stopped, I opened the front door to check our mail and an envelope dropped. It sailed to the concrete porch.

It was sealed, but lacked a name or address. The corner stuck out from the door was wet from the rain. I tucked it with the mail and took a seat on the couch as I went through all the bills, separating them from the junk. I finally got to it. A plain envelope. Twirling it in my hand I stared at it.

"What's that?" Eric asked as he strolled into the room.

"I don't know. It was stuffed in the door."

"That's odd. Probably nothing."

His voice was reassuring, but a flicker of fear rose in my chest. "Here, you open it. I'm going to start dinner preparations." I tossed him the letter and exited to the kitchen.

Moments later he joined me, leaned against the door frame. "You should see this." He held a blank piece of computer paper in his hand.

The letter was printed from a computer and all it said was 'I found you'. I let go of it as if it would bite me and the flicker of fear ignited. It was personal, meant for one of us. A whisper in my head said it was a message for me.

Eric pushed off the wall, his forehead wrinkled in worry. "Emily, it's weird, but probably just a prank."

Shallow breaths escaped my lips. "You're... you're probably right. That's it; a prank." I convinced my mind and shut down the whisper. It was nothing. Stupid kids.

He snaked his arms around my waist and kissed my cheek. "We can call the police. I'm sure they'd confirm other people in the neighborhood have gotten these same letters."

"No, I hate to waste their time over this. It's nothing."

A week later, the next letter came. Another blank envelope with a simple message typed and printed on a sheet of white computer paper: 'The time is soon'.

I called Eric, shaking in fear. The flame of dread reignited, moving through my chest and extremities.

"Calm down, Emily. Call the police. Call them now." The concern in Eric's voice prominent. "I'm leaving work now."

I clicked off the phone and dialed the police station. The officer arrived only moments before Eric pulled into the driveway.

A female cop. Her frame small and dark hair pulled into a tight pony tail that pulled at the skin on the sides of her face when she spoke. She dropped the letters into an evidence bag. "These have been going around the last couple weeks. They're probably pranks, nothing to be worried about, but we've increased the police presence in the neighborhood, hoping to catch them or deter them."

Her words were not reassuring, although they were meant to be. *Why would someone do this?* I asked myself the question. The officer seemed to have no idea, but did take the letters and said she'd get back to us if they turned up anything and to let them know if we received any more.

A neighborhood watch was brought together and, with the extra police presence, we hoped to catch or stop whoever the twisted mind was behind the letters, but they stopped on their own. A week went by, no letter. Another week went by and no letter. Nobody in the neighborhood had received any more. I sighed relief, assuming the worst was over. The flame of fear shrunk and life went back to normal.

The worst was not over.

Chapter 25

Rose of Death

Three weeks after the second letter, on a Saturday, we took the boys to the park and a picnic. The day was bliss until we got home. On the porch was a vase of black roses. My stomach dropped to the ground and vomit rose in my throat. I tried to swallow it down but wasn't successful. My lunch hit the dirt as I managed to swing my head to the side, missing the porch.

Eric called the police after settling me on the couch and sending the boys to their room. His words did nothing to reassure me the black roses were a prank. The quake in his voice gave away his own fear. A dark cloud settled on the room, promising to suffocate me.

The same female officer arrived at our house. Like the letter, she bagged the flowers and took them as evidence.

"Has anyone else received the black roses? Are the police doing anything about this?" Eric's voice shook with fear and anger.

"Mr. Turnwell, I understand how upset you are. The letters were checked for fingerprints and every one of them came up clean. No prints on the envelope or the letter. The black roses were also delivered to another home..." Her words hung as if she had more to say.

"My wife is pregnant. We have two boys. I'm terrified and will do whatever necessary to protect my family."

The officer took in a breath. "I can tell you, although you aren't alone, you are the only family who has received all the letters and the roses. I will personally drive by your house daily and will make a request to have the police detail in the neighborhood come by your house. As terrifying as this is, it isn't a crime and no harm has been done."

Eric nodded. "In other words, one of us has to be hurt before the police will step in." He threw his arms into the air.

"I'm doing everything I can." She handed him her card. "Call me if anything more happens."

"That's it!" Eric stormed out of the house and returned an hour later with a dog. Not a tiny puppy but a six-month-old Lab.

The boys took to the dog immediately and we named him Flash because he was so quick. I couldn't argue. A dog would alert us if anyone was prowling around the house and a pet was good for the boys.

The next afternoon I called Mike. It was the need to tell someone else, and Mike was my safety net. Eric would be mad. He was our family protector, but Mike was my bodyguard, and at the moment I needed to hear his voice. I spilled everything in almost one breath.

Anger, not fear, swelled in his voice. "Someone's stalking you! I'm coming over and staying there. No way someone's going to scare the shit out of my sister! No way. I'll kill him."

It wasn't the reaction I wanted, but it was the one I knew I would get. His protective need for me was the security I so badly needed. "Don't do that. What are you going to do that Eric won't? Besides, he'll be pissed I told you."

"No he won't, he'll understand."

Flash lay on the floor at my feet, napping, his chest moving in and out. "We have a dog now. If anyone tries to get into the house he'll alert us. "

"That's not good enough, Em. Prepare a room. I'll be there this weekend. No more discussion."

My brother was stubborn like a mule, like Eric. I married my brother. I'd never thought about it in those terms but they had so much in common. That weekend, I learned how much as they fitted our house with an alarm and cameras.

Mike spent the money he got from Aunt Carly on buying his own alarm company. His equipment was hanging all over our house. Mike and Eric were like two peas in a pod as they pulled wire through the attic and dropped it down the walls, programmed the box at the door, and fitted cameras on the exterior. They even set up a surveillance TV in our closet.

"Now you'll get him on camera," Mike offered as he cracked open a beer.

Eric took a swig of his. "How do you feel now?" he asked, his eyes fixed on me.

"Better." Truth was, I did feel better, but not because we had a state-of-the-art security system. It was having my two bodyguards together only feet from me and Flash at my side.

That night I cuddled next to Eric in bed and ran my palm over his five o'clock stubble. "I'm surprised at you."

"Yeah, why's that?"

"You accepted my brother's help and equipment. That stuff's not cheap."

"I know. I helped with the install so we got the equipment free but we'll be paying him monthly for the monitoring."

I let out a long sigh. "You stubborn ass!"

He smiled and guided a lock out of my face. "You know it!"

He slid his hands down my sides, tickling me, which brought laughter to my lips. His hands continued scooting until they were at my magic spot. He dove under the covers. "Time for dessert."

His mouth circled my clit and gently wiggled my knob until I was desperate for his cock. I couldn't help my moan as he entered. "Shh... your brother is here."

I chuckled. "Shut up and fuck me."

Chapter 26

Take Your Paci

Life settled into almost normalcy. Eric was confident in the security system and Flash -- except Flash barked at anybody outside the house, including kids playing in the neighborhood. We certainly knew when anyone was in the proximity of the house.

It was that moment when I almost let my guard down, almost forgot the shadows in the corners and footsteps in the hall, when my world crashed again. We were coming back from visiting with my parents. The boys came down from their sugar highs and were sleeping in the back, their gentle snores music to my ears. Eric and I were discussing life, the kids, the baby. Everything was just right.

The sky was clear and the quarter moon fully visible. I rolled my window halfway to take in the woodsy scent. My mind drifted into lala land with the boys, peace in my heart.

A loud beep woke me when Eric pressed his palm hard against the horn and a set of high headlights stared at us. Eric swerved the car off the road. It jerked and bumped before coming to a stop.

My heart drummed hard, my breath caught and immediately I gawked into the back seat. The boys were still strapped in tight but now waking.

"Eric. What happened, Eric?"

"Emily, it's fine. That guy in the truck wasn't watching his side of the road. Maybe he fell asleep." His voice more annoyed than anything.

"Eric, what if... what if?" I glanced at the boys again. "You don't think?"

"How are the boys? And no, I don't think. Just a reckless driver."

"They're fine."

It was probably too much of a stretch to think the stalker was driving the truck. I couldn't blame him or her for everything that had happened in our lives but the timing made it seem as though it was related. For the past couple months every time I thought life would be OK the stalker struck again.

He merged back onto the road and we arrived home safely, but that uneasy flicker in my gut flamed up. I didn't think it was a coincidence. I slept uneasy that night as murmurs spoke from the shadows.

Two weeks later, I came home from the grocery store and a white box was set against the garage door as if someone wanted us to see it; wanted *me* to see it. I kicked the box to the side of the garage beside the flower bed and left it, refusing to touch it. It could wait for Eric.

I laid down the realtor booklet I'd found in the shopping cart on the coffee table. It had a beautiful home in the country circled. There was plenty of land and space for the children. Moving might not be a bad idea and might be a way to rid our lives of the stalker. I'd show Eric when he got home, I thought as I stuffed the cereal and canned goods into the pantry, the white box on my mind. After finishing the groceries I stepped outside and stared at the box. There was no card. Then I remembered the cameras.

Rushing to the closet, I checked each one: nothing. Not a soul had come by our house but the mailman and he never walked up the driveway.

In a panic, I called Mike and told him about the package and how the cameras didn't catch anyone, as if the stalker was a ghost.

"Don't open that box. Call the police, have them do it, and call Eric. I'm on my way." His voice filled with trepidation.

I disconnected the call and immediately phoned the police then Eric, my voice shaking and my palms sweaty. A swat team arrived at our home, treating the box as if it had a bomb inside instead of a pink baby pacifier with the name Erin printed on a white bow around it. I felt stupid looking at the innocent baby item and I knew it would be the talk of the police station: *crazy pregnant woman freaks over baby pacifier.* Neither Mike, Eric, or myself laughed even a tiny bit.

I couldn't sit still and remembered the realtor booklet. I did a little research while Mike and Eric checked the cameras and feed. The cameras hadn't lied and the stalker wasn't a ghost. Mike found a glitch in the camera and took it with him. He'd bring a new one back and install it tomorrow. He assured us it was a common issue with that type of camera, but thought the company had resolved it. The one he was bringing to install didn't have that issue.

Once the boys were in bed, all my strength was zapped away and I was a scared little girl. Dark, sinister murmurs erupted in my head, all talking at one time so they were a blur. Eric was sitting on the edge of the couch, his body tense and senses on high. He immediately lifted his head and took me in with his eyes. I ran to him and wrapped my arms around his neck.

"Eric, we can't stay here. I don't feel safe." My voice quivered with each word.

"Honey." He folded his arms around me as I buried my head in his chest.

All my fears surfaced, even the ones I barely admitted to myself. "Since the first letter a pit of blackness sunk to my stomach, then the black roses, the truck running us off the road. Now a pink pacifier with the name Erin written on the bow. Who but us knows the baby's name? It's a simple pacifier, but it makes the butterflies in my stomach flap like they're on steroids!"

"I know." He caressed my hair.

I jerked my head upwards. "There is something dark in my past. I felt it since the first letter. I've never wanted to know about my biological family. The idea makes my heart flutter and scares the shit out of me. My parents fell in love with me from the first time they saw me and adopted me as soon as the courts allowed. Do you think… never mind." For a moment the idea my biological parents' murderer was out to get me and finish the job scooted across my brain, but that was ridiculous. I told myself that; convinced myself of that.

Eric rubbed his hand across his lips and mustache, a few hairs sprung upwards as his fingers brushed over them. "It's not safe here, but I don't yet know the solution. I hate for this freak to run us out of our own home."

I grabbed the realtor booklet off the coffee table. "Maybe we can move. I found this today in the grocery cart. I was going to throw it away, but the circled one caught my eye." I handed him the Chesterville real estate guide.

"Chesterville. That's a hike every day and no telling the psycho won't follow us." I was afraid his stubbornness and logic would get in the way.

"Can we at least look? In the mountains, away from all the freaks here in the city. I looked at the schools and they're better than anything here. The kids could grow up breathing fresh mountain air and watching the stars. I made an appointment with the realtor

Saturday." I pleaded with my eyes, begging him to consider.

He smoothed stray blond ringlets behind my ear. "I love you."

"Does that mean yes?" I searched his face.

"Yes. I'll stop at nothing for you and the boys." Those few words made me feel so much better. I snuggled onto his chest absorbing each beat of his heart.

Saturday, we set out for Chesterville to meet the realtor at Eighteen Eclipse Lane. The day was beautiful, the sky clear, and a gentle breeze keeping the air sweater weather.

"Hi, Mr. and Mrs. Turnwell." The realtor leaned forward, giving us each a quick shake. Her spiked heels seemed out of place for the mountain home with its gravel roads.

"Good morning, Mrs. Jarvis," offered Eric.

She stretched her lips into a forced grin. "You ready? As you can tell, the road is quiet, secluded, but only a few minutes from town. And the schools here are third in the state." She looked to the boys then my swollen belly.

I shrugged. "Ready."

We followed Mrs. Jarvis up the steps and into the house. "Wait till you see the view from the back deck. Uh… it's breathtaking. And there's plenty of space. Four bedrooms including a spacious master, one for each of your boys, and a nursery." She droned on, showing each room and feature in the house from the stainless steel appliances to the master suite spa tub.

The boys exchanged glances with each other as they eyed the custom swing set in the backyard. "Dad, can we play?" asked Ethan.

Eric nodded. "Go, test it out."

"What do you think?" asked Mrs. Jarvis.

I loved the house and turned to Eric to get an idea of his thoughts. His expression said it all with his partial smile and the faraway look in his eye. I knew he was considering it.

He swallowed. "Mrs. Jarvis, we love the house, but need to discuss this as a family. We'll give you a call."

"Did I mention the owner is letting it go at a bargain? He hoped to use it as a home away from home getaway, but recently learned he'll be leaving the country indefinitely and so needs to sell as soon as possible."

We arrived home late in the evening after spending the rest of the day enjoying quality time at Bouncy Kingdom. While the boys played, we talked about the house. I'd gotten used to Flash greeting us at the door and was taken back when he didn't come running, but even dogs needed sleep.

I ushered the boys upstairs and tucked them in, kissing each of their foreheads. They shared a room, the baby -- no longer Erin -- would have her own, but it would be nice if they all had their own, especially with Ethan eight years old now.

"Night." I flipped the light off, blew kisses, and closed the door, leaving it cracked so the hall nightlight could shine into their room.

Eric sat on the couch, his brows creased into a V. I immediately recognized Eric's trouble face. "Not again. No." Panic bubbled in my gut, blackness sprung from the corners and glided toward me.

He swallowed hard then cleared his throat. "It's Flash."

Water puddled in the corner of my eyes. "What do you mean 'Flash'?"

"We're making an offer on that house and then we'll figure out how."

A steady stream of tears rolled down my cheeks. "What's wrong with Flash?" I padded towards the kitchen.

He shook his head, jumping off the couch to block my path. "No!"

From the corner of my eye, I spotted a matt of hair covered in blood. Losing it completely I pummeled Eric's chest with my fists. He pulled me to him and we walked to the couch. "What did the bastard do?" I asked, heat and fear rising in my voice.

He sucked in a deep breath. "He mutilated him."

That was it. The very last straw. I wasn't spending another night in that house. "We are out of here. Pack the car; we're going to my parents!" I shouted, my fear taking control of the situation.

That night, after the police left, Eric buried Flash. I watched him from the window, knowing exactly what was on his mind as dirt clods flew through the air. The same thoughts that were on mine. Each time we called the police, filed a report, and no results -- nothing. The creep left no trace. He patted the dirt over Flash's mangled body and marched back to the house.

The car already packed, we headed to my parents. The following day, we made an offer on the house.

The next evening, Eric and I sifted through our finances. It wasn't that he didn't make decent money and we had equity in our current home, but two mortgages were impossible. "We have to do this. Maybe my…"

Eric interrupted. "Your parents."

I nodded. His words made me feel small and guilty for even bringing up the suggestion. They had plenty of Aunt Carly's money still.

He lifted his head to the ceiling, raking his fingers through his thinning hair. Lowering his head, he looked into my eyes. The stress was getting to him, bags hung beneath his eyes and deep wrinkles stretched across his forehead. He took my hands in his. "I only want their help as a last resort." Eric worked hard for everything he earned in life. Unlike me, his family was poor. He made straight As to get into college on a scholarship. He never took handouts, but his family had to come before his pride.

My fingers wiggled in his hands. "I've told my parents everything. They only want us all to be safe." I wiped the tears trickling over my cheek.

"I'm scared too. All I want is my family safe." His quivering voice gave away his own fear. "We can do this and we'll ask them *if* we need help."

I nodded and feared Eric staying at the home alone all week while he worked. My parents' home was just too far for his daily commute.

"Can you stay with Lucas?" Lucas was Eric's longtime friend. We didn't see him as much as Eric would have liked but I was sure, under the circumstances, he'd let him crash on their couch.

"Would you feel better if I did?"

"Yes. We shouldn't ever go back to that house."

Eric bolted upright with excitement. "Maybe we can rent it?"

I shook my head back and forth, fear rising in my throat. "No. I want no connection. If we rent, then we have to check on the place, our names, our new address will be tied to the house."

"We can go through a rental agency. They take care of everything."

"No. This stalker… whoever he or she is… is smart, calculating. I want a clean break." I was convinced it wasn't the garage camera that malfunctioned and I think, after finding Flash, we all agreed. There was no footage of anyone breaking into our home. The camera was covered with tape that I was sure had no prints on it.

His eyes drifted to my belly then he padded behind me, tripping on a Lincoln Log. "What the…" He picked up the toy and it pinged as it hit the table where he dropped it. He snaked his arms around my neck, laying gentle kisses over my cheek. "You're right. I'm a proud man and if we can't figure this out -- if we can't sell the house right away -- we'll ask your parents."

His kisses worked their way to my lips. I parted my mouth, accepting his tongue.

A week after our house went on the market it sold. A very generous offer, making it possible to get the loan and have plenty of money for our down payment. It worked out; a sure sign this was meant to be and the stalker would be a thing of the past. A memory I'd never revisit.

Three months later, we closed the deal on our new home and moved to Eighteen Eclipse Lane in Chesterville. The horrific incidents ceased and our lives became peaceful.

The nursery barely ready, baby Erica
made her entrance into the world.

Chapter 27

The Edge

Loud crashes echoed through the darkness; glass breaking and bodies tumbling. I was stuck somewhere between life and death. It was like a horrifying nightmare and I couldn't will myself out of it. My eyelids were like sandbags and my mind groggy.

Something was dragging across the floor. The lids of my eyes refused to open and my mouth was dry. I tried to move it, to say something, but it was stuck. My body tingled and I pushed my mouth with my tongue. It felt strange, not part of me, soft but not fleshy. Fabric. There was fabric in my mouth. I couldn't swallow and drool pooled from the corners of my mouth. Feeling, sensation, was returning.

My mind stuck in replaying my past. All the memories on the precipice of my mind completed the broken mirror as footfalls moved through the house. The same ones, the same gait, only larger now and moving through *my* house. Every night, I curled into a ball just like the tiny girl balled under her dresser with her favorite blanket. I was there when my family was killed.

I knew the killer!

Part 3

Enlightenment

Chapter 28

Diseased Blood

The dark memories of my life coalesced. All the whispers and murmurs in my mind grew loud as I absorbed each word.

The killer will be out soon.

Maybe. We have to tell her... one day.

My brother was a lowlife, and Philmonia wasn't any better, but Carly isn't like that. She's not.

You look like Dad.

My father was my uncle! My biological father married Aunt Carly's niece, Philmonia -- my biological mother. That's why we looked alike.

It's been over five years since he got out and nothing. He was a kid, a mixed up kid, and nobody knows if he was even guilty.

Who else? The house wasn't broken into. It had to be that twisted fuck.

Home invasion. Aunt Carly's niece killed in a home invasion. My parents killed in a home invasion. It was the same. Not a coincidence. The children in the pictures. The little blond girl and the two boys. My biological brothers and myself. The oldest one -- the part I tore from the picture and burned, watching his face melt away.

The voices buzzed across my brain and one word stuck out: *Evan, Evan.* It repeated. Evan, my oldest brother. The picture I burned. Evan was here now. He killed our family and now it was my turn. My death.

I'd never liked Evan. He'd always scared me and those eyes, his eyes, blue with shimmers of green and deep black shadows that moved across them. When I'd seen the picture, the memory tried to surface but my subconscious squashed it as it did every memory, every clue, in my life.

My biological father always yelling at Evan and strong arms carrying me somewhere; then my parents now. The ones who raised me, saved me from a life of horror and dysfunction. I opened my eyes and stared into the blackness that moved in waves over Evan's corneas. He killed them!

"You little ass!" Evan's voice thundered.

My hands tied behind my back, my legs tied at the ankles, a sock in my mouth, I couldn't move or scream. I watched in horror, my pulse thumping so hard it echoed in my ears. A blade ripped across Ethan's throat. My precious little boy. I couldn't do anything to save him. My heart ripped in two, my will bottomed out. I was next, but where was little Erica?

I shifted my eyes across the room, searching for something to free myself, to save what was left of my family and gagged into the sock at what I saw. Eric, slumped in a chair, his head drooped and pointed towards the floor. *Was he alive?*

Ethan's head slumped and blood poured over his still chest. A scream erupted, curdling the blood in my body. My youngest son -- Elian.

He was alive! I wiggled, urging my muscles to respond, forcing them to do something. I pulled my hands, attempting to squeeze them through their bindings. *Too late!*

Evan ripped the blade across Elian's neck, his head drooped and blood sputtered and discharged over his tiny chest. I couldn't breathe, my nose stuffy from the onslaught of tears. The sock made it impossible for me to catch my breath.

Where was Erica? My little baby. *Where was she?* I didn't see her in the bloodbath of my kitchen. There was a chance she was alive. *Breathe, Emily!* I willed my nose to take in as much air as possible. I had to get to her. I worked my feet and hands trying to free them. Something worked, the chair toppled. A sharp pain radiated through my brain as my head hit the floor.

"What do you think of the house? I picked it out for you. It's secluded. You can scream but no one will hear you." His voice so calm, as if we were having a conversation about the weather and I wasn't surrounded in chaos and blood. My family's blood as their dead eyes looked down on me.

It was all my fault for never finding my family, asking the questions, listening to the conversations. *It was my fault!* They didn't deserve to die for my stupidity, my ignorance. I barely saw his face through the tears pouring from my eyes like a never-ending rain.

He pulled the sock from my mouth. I gasped for each breath, air filling my lungs again.

"Go ahead," he challenged.

"Why? Why are you doing this?" I asked, my voice small and shaky.

A smile crept over his face. I remembered that smile. It hadn't changed. "Because I can. It started to keep Mommy away. I killed her eight times and still she came back." His eyes grew large and a black fog moved over the iris. "Then I met someone and she went away. Poof, that was it! Now I'm doing it because I enjoy it. I want you to feel the pain I felt every time she touched me." His voice suddenly sinister as he growled out the last few words.

He walked towards Eric, reading the horror in my eyes as he ripped the blade fast and quick across his neck, his murky eyes glaring into my soul. I couldn't watch, squeezing my eyes tight, to avoid the inevitable horror. *Erica! My little girl. Why didn't I ever ask about my past?*

"She never harmed you. She would have hurt Elfred. That was mercy. It had to be done, but you…" He grabbed a fistful of my hair. I whimpered as pain surged through my neck, tears streaking my cheeks. "You were special."

"I don't remember. I was a baby. I didn't. I…" He stuffed the sock back in my mouth as I screamed those few words.

Holding the blade against my flesh, he twisted slowly. I whimpered and closed my eyes, waiting for the sting that would end my life.

"I, I, I, That's always been it. I, you… You care only for yourself! Open your eyes!" he seethed, mimicking me.

I was a baby. I didn't know anything but my little world. He was insane! How can a tiny child know anything of selfishness? I popped my eyes open on his command. My only thought as Evan's blade, cold and stiff, rested against my throat: *Erica, sweet baby.*

A sting erupted from my neck as Evan twisted the blade further. He slashed again and again. My body grew numb and sank into darkness.

Chapter 29

Mom

I jolted awake, expecting to see Eric in bed next to me. Instead, I was on the kitchen floor with a vague memory of a heart-pounding nightmare, my brain unable to register the events of it. Tears ran in streams down my cheeks and my heartbeat thumped in my ears.

I swallowed to catch my breath. An unease gathered in my gut; something didn't feel right. I was on the kitchen floor and the house was still, too still. The stars and moon blotted out by the clouds hindered my view. Standing with caution, my heart wild in my chest, I walked to the cabinets and pulled out our utility drawer and grabbed the flashlight.

I pressed the button and nothing happened. Hitting it a couple times against my hand, it still didn't respond. I set it down and went for a candle. The flame of the match burned bright then died as I brought it to the wick. I tried a few more times and it caught, creating a glow that gave me a few feet of vision.

I crept through the house, the feeling of unease growing stronger with each step. When I reached my oldest boy's room, the unease grew into fear. I swallowed it down and pushed the door open. Without enough light to see the bed, I moved closer to it. A lump in the center took away my breath. *Breathe, Emily,* I recited in my head.

When the candle's light reached the bed, I gasped. It was empty. The lump was a pillow. "Ethan," I called. The response was deafening silence.

Rushing to my youngest boy's room, I pushed the door open and flew to the bed. It was empty. I rushed to Erica's crib -- empty. My fear grew into full panic and I rushed into my room. No Eric. My family was gone!

I ran outside and through the woods, calling. There were no house lights, the stars and moon absent from the sky. Branches cut and scraped the skin on my arms and legs. Rocks dug into the soles of my bare feet. "Eric!"

Breathless, I stopped and spun in a slow circle. I wasn't in the woods behind my house anymore. I didn't recognize where I was. Wilting into a lump on the ground, I cried myself to sleep. The nightmare came again. The sensation of falling jolted me awake. My eyes opening to darkness everywhere and the echo: *You stupid girl.*

"Emily." A hand rocked against my side. "Emily dear, wake up."

I opened my eyes to morning sunshine and heavenly blue eyes. "Mom?"

"You were having a bad dream. Come, let's get you breakfast."

Strands of blond hair, purposely left out of the updo, framed her face. "Where is everyone?"

Her manicured brows formed a V. "Who, honey?"

And I couldn't remember; vague flashes dissipated. "No one."

There was something and someone I should remember but couldn't.

My mother pulled back the sheer pink curtains and opened the blinds. More sun filtered into the room. My bed was decorated with pink ruffles and polka dots. A large white dollhouse embellished in detail was displayed on a table. None of this felt like my room.

"Breakfast won't eat itself, Emily," called my mother.

I scrambled out of bed, unable to push the awkward sensation that something wasn't right out of my head. I became disoriented expecting to walk straight down the hall and make a right into the kitchen. Across from my room was a bathroom. To my right was the end of the hall and a door. I opened the door to find a linen closet. There was another door to my left. I pushed it open to my mother's room. Turning on my heel I went the other direction. There were two more rooms. I pressed my hand against one of the doors to open it.

"Emily?" My mother stretched her hand over mine. "This way, honey."

I walked with her, watching the door from the corner of my eye. On the kitchen table was a pitcher of orange juice and a plate with croissants and strawberries. Two plates were set across from each other. Through the open curtain was the street. It was empty.

I ate my breakfast studying my surroundings. They were vaguely familiar. It was odd. I lived here; I should know my way around the house.

It seemed we shouldn't be alone in the house. "Where is everyone?" I asked.

My mother took a deep breath, her expression one of seriousness. "It's been hard for you, for both of us." She reached her hand across the table. When I didn't reach back she came around behind me and wrapped her arms around my shoulders. "Everything will be OK." Her words were soft, as if to ease me.

"What's wrong with me?"

She kissed my head. "Oh sweetie, nothing is wrong with you. You had a very bad dream is all."

The idea I was somewhere I didn't belong filled my gut. My mother wasn't even familiar, yet I knew she was my mother.

The flowery scent of freesia drifted past me. I inhaled deeply, allowing the aroma into my body and soul. It was familiar like déjà vu. I inhaled again to catch the odor and attach it to a memory, but the moment was lost.

"I know what will make you feel better." My mom glanced at me with a smile. "Come on!" Like a giddy teen she took my hand and pulled me with her. In her room was a large vanity with gold trim, stacked with beauty supplies, makeup, and hair products. She insisted I sit. When I looked in the mirror I expected to find a woman and saw a teenager instead.

She grabbed my hair from the back and a brush, pulling it through my hair. The curls sprung back into place. "How old am I, Mom?"

Her eyes focused on my head as she styled my hair and answered, "That's a silly question. You're fourteen."

The surreal moment became more surreal. Fourteen. It seemed I hadn't been fourteen for many years but, glancing at myself in the mirror, she was right.

After brushing makeup on my eyes and cheeks she asked, "Well, what do you think?"

"It's nice." I turned my head to get a better look at myself and my hair. I glanced down at my clothes. I was wearing a baby blue dress with lace that wrapped around my neckline and arms. *When had I changed my clothes?*

We never left the house. Each day went by almost the same. Each night I had the same nightmare without any memory of it. To keep track I wrote bits and pieces of it in a journal and tucked the journal in a safe spot. I punched a hole through the fabric on the underside of the bed's box springs and stuffed the journal onto the wooden frame.

I woke early and reached under the bed for my journal. My hand brushed against something soft. I pulled out a pink blanket. It smelled like baby powder. The blanket hadn't been there before. I snuggled it in my arms, taking in the sweet scent. I closed my eyes and saw a baby face framed in blond ringlets.

"Emily." My mother's voice broke the moment and I stuffed the blanket beneath my covers as she opened the door.

Each day started with breakfast, followed by doing my hair and face. A different dress appeared on me by the time she was finished. It was like a teenage slumber party on repeat.

The pink blanket didn't leave my mind as a new dress appeared on me and I gazed at myself in the vanity mirror. Following my mother out of the room a little boy with blond curls ran past me. "Catch me, Emily!" He giggled and disappeared into the living room. A man with dark hair lay snoring in the recliner.

"Dad, Elfred?" I veered into the room. They glanced at me and vanished. Anger boiled in me. My mom lied. *Where were my brother and father?*

I charged into the kitchen where she hummed as she sliced vegetables for salad. "Where is Dad?"

She dropped the knife. Her eyes narrowed and lips straightened, then drew into her usual painted smile. "He's gone sweetie."

"Elfred too?!" I didn't hide the emotion in my voice.

She nodded. "Sit down."

"No. What happened to them?" The words burst from my mouth, cracking the silence in the air.

"They were in a car wreck and so were you. The car flipped and they died on impact but you," she walked towards me and grabbed my hands, "you survived. The doctors said your memory would return."

I pulled my hands from her grip.

"Honey, you're remembering. This is good. In fact, lets celebrate." She ran back to the counter and slid the knife and cutting board into the sink. They landed with a ping.

"Can we go outside?" The sun was especially bright that day and I longed to feel it on my skin.

Ignoring my question, her face lit up. "We'll make a chocolate cake."

"No, I want to leave."

"Honey, it's going to storm. Today isn't a good day for outdoor activities."

Thunder roared and lightning cut through the suddenly foreboding sky. It had been sunny only moments earlier.

The rain carried on all day and into the night. I heard footfalls in the hall and peered under my door as two shadows passed. Getting up from my bed, the sweet, pink baby blanket in my hand, I pushed my door open gently so as not to make a sound and watched my mom and a boy, older than Elfred, enter her room. She closed the door behind them. I slipped closer to her room and pressed my head against the door. Their voices were too quiet to make out their conversation.

A sudden chill ran down my spine and I backed away from the door and continued backing until a patch of warm air passed through me. A person manifested from the heat. His dark hair, eyes, and muscular build halted me in my tracks. Like my father and Elfred, he didn't see me. I reached out to touch him and my hand went through him.

He rubbed his arm where I'd tried to touch. "Emily."

Chapter 30

Death is Only the Beginning

His voice triggered something inside me and I remembered. "Mike," I called, a flood of memories circulating in my head. My brother. I'd grown up with him.

"Emily." Hands shook me and I stared again into my mother's face. I jolted upward, my eyes searching but only finding my pink room.

"Honey, it was a bad dream again."

I stared into her cerulean eyes. Something about my life, the house, my dreams, didn't seem right. It was all wrong. I swallowed. Her gaze drifted to the pink blanket wrapped in my hand.

"What's this?" she asked, taking it from me.

Anxiety and fear climbed into my throat and I couldn't speak.

"It needs a good washing." She left the room with it.

I followed. I didn't want the fresh baby powder scent washed away. It made me see the cute little girl, if only for brief seconds. There was something about her I needed to remember. "Please don't!" I reached for the blanket.

She drew it away. "It's dirty, honey, and needs to be washed."

I caught the end of the blanket and grabbed. She tugged harder, petals of freesia fell through the air and the blanket dropped to the floor which turned into the surface of a lake. It shattered as the blanket hit it, sending ripples to the shore.

I plummeted beneath the surface of the lake. My mom called after me, "Emily, stay. Don't go. Don't leave me!" Her voice sounding long and stretched the further beneath the surface I drifted.

The water vanished, replaced by a dark vortex. My body spun and my mom's voice was replaced by a man and nasty words. *You guilty bitch! You killed your family!* echoed like thunder swirling with me, moving through me.

This was my dream. The one I kept having but couldn't remember. It was happening. I tried to wake myself and wished for my mom to call for me and pull me out of the dark place.

Images of death and my family slain, crimson rivers, a shiny silver object running across their necks over and over. *You dumb, guilty bitch!*

"Stop!" I screamed, remembering everything, but the sound dissipated in the vortex of doom. I covered my ears. It didn't stop the verbal assault. *You're the dumbest blond bitch. You, you, all by yourself, killed your family. They're dead! You'll never see them again. Your skin and muscle will boil from your bones and the fires will turn your bones to ash. You're going to the center of HELL!*

"No, stop, no, I didn't know. STOP!" My voice went nowhere. The words sucked into the vacuum. Tears didn't fall from my eyes and my nose didn't snot, but my soul cried for my family as I watched the blade run across their necks over and over. Evan's eyes clouded and black as tar. His glare ate at my soul.

The vortex rushed to a stop and my body stayed suspended in blackness. Footsteps swarmed from all directions then centered in one spot like millions of rats all converging on a single prey. They surrounded me then flames erupted in a circle around a single man. As he moved towards me the flames continued to loop and move with him.

His blond hair lay in waves and his face was a long oval with a pointed chin. His build lean and tall. As he grew closer his eyes became visible. They were an unnatural shade of green that emanated an emerald light. "You really are a dumb bitch."

He moved around my floating body that was completely numb, making it impossible to physically feel anything and impossible to turn and watch him. I opened my mouth but nothing came out.

"Emily, Emily. Really, you could have saved them or at least put up a fight. You never were curious. Lost in your own little perfect world." He came back around and faced me.

His hand moved towards my face but I couldn't feel his touch.

"You missed the memo that ignorance is no excuse and you paid the price. Your family paid the price."

A screen dropped down between me and him. Eric lay on the floor in a pool of his own blood, my boys' heads drooped, sitting bloodied and limp on the kitchen chairs. *Erica! Where was Erica?*

"Don't worry, little Erica is just fine. It wouldn't have been proper to kill her, she'll have her day. Maybe she won't be stupid like you and will seize the moment."

The movie screen lifted upwards and disappeared into the blackness. The flames surrounding him flared like a wall between us then receded, returning to the way they were.

Who are you? I thought, unable to speak.

"Your worst nightmare! That's who I am. Your mother made me possible!" The words roared through my ears like a freight train shaking the invisible ropes suspending me.

I thought of my mother, the house, my pink room. The boy she took into her bedroom. My mother did bad things to him. I didn't understand as a child. I did now. That little boy was my older brother. She abused him so badly he turned against her.

"She was an evil bitch who will never rest!" His voice roared around me.

You hear my thoughts?

"Like I said, you're a dumb bitch. It took you long enough to figure that out. You are in my world now." He chuckled then sighed, straightening his lips he continued his verbal assault. "I guess I have to spell it out. Once upon a time, a young boy who was *never* born found a home inside a creature innocent and pure. The problem was the little homeless boy wasn't alone. He had to share it with two others. One a whimpering scaredy cat like you."

He released his hand in the air displaying a man in a corner surrounded by flames, his face impossible to see as it was buried in his knees. His body convulsed as if crying. Blond curls covered his head. When he dropped his hand the image went away.

He drew up his other arm. Another man surrounded by flames licking at his body appeared. "The other strong and merciless, yet strict in ritual."

He withdrew his hand and stomped. "I'm what bound them together!" His demonic voice boomed through the darkness. "The thread that binds. I'm unstoppable!"

The emerald flames in his eyes erupted. "If you're lucky you will meet my sister, our mother, when she tries to save your putrid, weak little soul. We cannot die. We have a choice. She made that possible for us. We are one and the same now." His words a riddle I didn't know how to untangle. *Who was this person that was both mother and sister?* He disappeared with a satanic chuckle that resonated through the darkness and through me.

An image of myself, bloodied and lying across the kitchen floor. My family weren't the only ones that were dead. So was I.

Chapter 31

Invisible

My eyes flickered open and I was standing in my kitchen. Erica was balled in the corner, whimpering, her face covered in a mess of snot and tears. A black shadow swarmed her, tendrils of darkness stretched towards her. "Get away from her!" I shouted and grabbed for the shadow but it dissipated, followed only by a wicked chuckling, and I was alone.

It was only a vision. An unsettling feeling gripped me, becoming stronger as I peered at the sheets covering the table and chairs. At first my mind didn't process that I was only seeing a vision. *Where did she go and where was the rest of my family?* I flew through the house, checking every room, calling for them, but I was alone.

It was like a strange dream and I'd lost time somewhere. *Had I been drugged?* I glanced downward and realized my feet weren't exactly on the floor but hovering above it. The floor visible through my legs, my chest, my arms.

You stupid bitch. You let them die! resounded in my brain and I dropped to the floor in a heap. Sharp, phantom pains erupted from my neck as the man with the dark eyes, my biological brother, sliced through my neck.

The memories of their deaths rushed through me and the man in the black vortex. The flames fluid around him. *I was dead! They were dead!*

Erica! I had to get to Erica. If the man told the truth, she was alive. She would not suffer my fate and that of her father and brothers. It would be my mission as a... a... spirit... a ghost, to force her memories, never give up. My body floating over the surface, it felt no physical pain but my soul was heavy. The sensation and emotions coursed through my translucent form.

I stared once more at my house. All the furniture covered. *How long had I been trapped with my mom and in the darkness? Why was I able to return?* It felt long, but my guess was time worked different in eternity than on Earth. I flowed through the brick wall and smiled as memories of my boys running on the lawn, sliding on the grass through the sprinklers, surged through the electrical impulses controlling me.

That's all I was now; impulses and whatever was left of my physical body, nothing more than a series of chemical reactions. The logic in the situation didn't change it. I was dead, my family was dead, all but Erica and I needed to find her. Maybe that's why I had returned -- to save her precious soul.

A woman walked by me. Her shoulder-length coffee-colored hair bounced with her steps. The sun was high but its radiance didn't touch me. I walked beside the woman. "Can you help me?"

She swatted at her neck where my words landed as if they were pesky mosquitoes. I touched her arm. My fingers went through her. She swatted her arm. I poked around her body, back, legs, neck. She swatted each time, telling me she couldn't see me but she could feel me.

Wrapping her arms around her chest as if she couldn't feel the sun through a cold breeze, she spun around searching the air then ran away. I spooked her. When the revelation became evident I couldn't help but chuckle. There was no invisible veil between us.

Hundreds, thousands, maybe millions, of spirits like me roamed the earth completely invisible to the human eye. We occupied the same realm yet they couldn't see us.

A rumble of voices and whispered words moved through the air, breaking the silence. *I need to find my husband. Where is my son? Have you seen him? Where am I? Can you help me?* It was too much and cluttered my thoughts but I couldn't make it stop. The chatter grew into an undecipherable buzz that stayed with me.

Finding Erica was no easy task and I didn't know where to start. The problem was, I couldn't remember much past our ugly deaths and my afterlife, so my wandering was aimless at best. With no idea of time, days stretched on into weeks, months, years. I didn't know. Maybe only seconds. And the constant buzz of chattering lost spirits was always present.

Chapter 32

Vines of Mortality

Returning to my home was maybe the best way for me to find her. Sun glinted through the windows of the empty home that once housed my happy family. Elian ran past me, a stuffed dog in his hands, laughing as his brother tackled him to the ground. They rolled and giggled as he tossed the dog. "Catch it, Erica."

The buzzing of spirit voices droned into silence as I lost myself in the memories of my family.

She didn't appear or answer. The dog sailed into the unknown. Next Eric was relaxing on the couch, flashes from the screen lit up the dark room. I lay on his lap as he smoothed my hair and twisted my curls. It was so real, I almost felt it. Embracing each memory, I enveloped myself in them, but something was always missing -- Erica. These were only memories of my deceased family. Erica was still out there. The house gave me few clues, but it gave me comfort.

Time passed. The trees lost their leaves, snow covered the ground, and still no Erica. *Where was she?* Remembering I had to find her, I searched the house, trying hard to ignore the memories enveloping me. Her room was a void. No toys or dresser. No clothes, not even... I tried hard to grasp the memory before it faded. Not even her pink blanket. Her chubby cheeks and fingers flashed through my head so quick I barely saw her. There was nothing in the house of hers.

I couldn't grasp and hold onto anything physically so I moved through the furniture coverings. Plenty of pictures sat on tables and shelves. After spending long minutes or so staring at them, I began to remember little pieces. I was looking at my family, my parents and brothers and Eric's sister and mother. The pictures told me nothing about how to find my child.

Maybe the house wasn't the answer to finding Erica. It was then the door opened and a gentleman walked in. A large leather-covered notepad and a pen in his hand. He lifted the coverings and made notes of the furniture. *What was he doing?*

How could I ask him? I couldn't. Instead, I remembered the girl I spooked and hoped it would work on him. I walked through him, poked him, punched his arms. His eyes darted like crazy as he touched every part of him I touched.

"What are you doing?" I whispered.

"Is someone there?" he responded, his eyes wide as he moved closer and closer to the door.

"I am. What are you doing?" I screamed.

He visibly shivered then bolted through the front door, not turning back. His car flew down the gravel road, rocks and dust flying.

I didn't get answers, but maybe he wouldn't be back.

By the time the flowers bloomed, an SUV, traveled the gravel road outside my house, turning into the driveway. A man, his chest solid and large, stepped out of the vehicle. He turned and I recognized him. My brother Mike. A woman came around the vehicle, her dark hair unfamiliar, but when she faced me I realized I knew her. My best friend Lori.

"Are you sure you want to do this?" she asked.

He nodded. "The man I hired refuses to come back in the house or send in his crew. He probably read the papers and got spooked."

She wrapped an arm around him. "I'm sorry. There are other people you can hire."

His voice low and mournful. "No. I need to do this and I'm grateful you're here to help." He turned and caught her in his embrace and kissed her lips.

She withdrew from his kiss and tilted her head. "I love you, Mike, don't forget that. I'm here for you."

I followed Mike through the house as he finished uncovering the furniture and went through our things. He carried in boxes and they packed clothes, dishes, anything that wasn't of personal value.

I caressed his back while he was leaning forward stacking clothing into a box. He twitched. "Mike," I whispered in his ear.

He twitched again. "Em. Are you here?"

I grabbed his hands, but mine went through his. I wanted nothing more than his strong arms around me, telling me this was all a bad dream.

He stood, his eyes searching the room. "Em?"

I hovered, my face only inches from him. "Do you hear me?"

"Em, if you're here, I miss you every day and pray you don't hate me. I could have done more. I should have done more. I'm so sorry." A tear followed by another dropped on his cheek and rolled.

A flash memory seized me. I was hiding behind a tree, peeking my head around the trunk. "Em," called a voice and a little boy darted around the tree.

"Found you." He tagged my arm. Now you're it!" He ran off. A flood of memories gripped me. He watched over me, protected me. At Aunt Carly's he gave me the courage to snoop through her house. The surveillance cameras at my house. He placed them everywhere. He couldn't know. I didn't know.

"Mike. I'm here, Mike. I know you did all you could. I love you!" My words went unheard. The man in the vortex; he only heard me through my mind, maybe it would work the same way here. I thought the words, attaching them to images as I pressed my palm against his back. It went through him. I sent all my memories of Erica to him. My little girl. I didn't know how, but there was something I needed to do to save her from a hidden force. The urges pushed through the impulses that held me together. There was something I had to do.

He turned and faced me as if he knew I was there, but his eyes stared through me, searching the room. "Don't worry, Erica is safe. I will never let anything happen to her, ever."

Did he hear me? Had I somehow communicated with him? "Where is she, Mike?" I asked, sending images of her as I pressed again on his back.

"Who are you talking to? Is someone here?" Lori walked into the room, bombarding him with questions and slicing our moment. I had more to send him as I grasped the moment.

"No."

She wiped the tear on his cheek. "This isn't your fault. Don't you dare blame yourself."

He nodded, but his face wasn't convincing.

I walked through her and between them. If I were alive we'd be touching.

She shivered. "It's chilly in here. I need a sweater."

He stepped forward, right through me, and rubbed his hands on her arms. "It is a bit cold. We can turn on the heat if you like."

She nodded. "Erica sometimes reminds me of her. That cute little dimpled smile and her bouncy little curls. Her hair is really getting thick and hard to brush." She chuckled.

"Today she hid under the coffee table when I mentioned the word brush."

Mike placed a blanket over her shoulders. "She's got personality. How did you coax her out?"

Lori's lips curled into a smile. "Chocolate cereal."

They both chuckled. Her laughter brought more memory flashes. They were never close until now. My death must have brought them together and they sat in front of me remembering moments in my life. I listened, soaking it all in, each word making each memory more real. I felt more and more like a person than a ghost.

They spent the night in mine and Eric's bed, snuggled with each other. I didn't sleep, so I watched them as if I was their guardian angel. In her sleep, I caressed Lori's hair, focusing on the memories I had of the two of us. If it worked on Mike, maybe it would work on her too. "You were always my best friend. I love you," I whispered the words into her ear.

She jolted out of bed and I sunk back to the foot, her eyes wide and frozen on me. She punched Mike in the shoulder. "Mike, Mike!" she called as she lifted out of bed and walked towards me. Her eyes searched mine.

He lifted his head. "Lori?"

"She's here. She was here. Right here, a second ago." She occupied the spot at the foot of the bed, exactly where I'd been.

He shook his head. "That's impossible."

"I know, but I swear I saw her. Only for a second, but I saw her."

She dropped onto the bed. Mike climbed forward and caressed her shoulders. "I thought I heard her earlier. It's crazy, but maybe being here in her house, the house she..." He swallowed hard. "It's our memories playing tricks."

How? How did she see me and why didn't she see me now? I was only a few feet from her. I tried to think about what was different from that moment to this one. I'd been talking to her, touching her, maybe that was it. That had to be it.

The following day they packed the big SUV, hauling box after box. I watched. I was going with them. They'd take me to Erica. The more time I spent with them, the more human I felt. My memories stuck like glue and brought me out of the dismal reality of death. The constant hum of other ghosts became a quiet buzz.

I floated with them, hiding in plain sight in the SUV. As it rolled down the road, being with them, the memories continued to pour in. We swept past trees and small towns, the regions becoming less mountainous until the vehicle stopped outside a townhome, its brick front inviting, with two large windows on the bottom floor and French doors opening to a balcony on the top.

I followed them up the steps to the wooden door surrounded by glass with an ivy design on the edges. Mike stuck the key in the lock and turned. He stepped inside, followed by Lori. As I reached the door's threshold a hand touched my back.

I turned around and my biological mother, the one who trapped me in the house with the pink room, gazed into my eyes. "Don't go in there."

"Why not?"

"It's a trap."

I pushed against her chest. "Like you. In that fake world, where every day was the same!" I seethed.

Her eyes narrowed and a dark shadow overcame her. "I was keeping you safe. From this. From these people!"

"No, no." I shook my head, determined to go through the door and find my little girl. I had to save her from something.

The door closed as I pulled up a leg to walk through it. A bright light enveloped me, carrying me with it. "No!" I screamed and ran towards the house, always moving further away. My mother had been right. It was a trap.

Chapter 33

Spirit Talker

I landed back in my kitchen. I didn't even get the chance to see my little baby before the strange force pulled me away. *Was I bound to this house forever? Was it my ghostly prison? Or, was my mother right, and it was a trap?*

A voice startled me. "You're a difficult ghost to find."

I jolted my head upward and stared at the most intriguing woman. Spirals of platinum hair hung against her cheeks and over her shoulders. Her eyes, one amber the other green, stared at me. "You see me?" was all I could think to say. Lori had seen me, but only for a second. This woman stared directly at me as if I wasn't a ghost any longer. Erica pushed to the back of my mind.

She nodded.

"You brought me back here!" I said, anger in my voice.

"I did. I've been searching for you and thought maybe you'd moved on or had become..." her words hung, "... a wanderer. This was my last effort."

I gasped as I studied my kitchen. Candles and stones were laid out and the air smelled like a strange herbal mix. "You trapped me!"

She gave me a warm smile that I wanted to knock right off her face. "I wouldn't call it a trap. You need to move on into the peaceful beyond and I can help you."

Her words triggered something I'd heard before. The man in the darkness with the unreal green eyes; 'If you're lucky you will meet my sister, our mother, when she tries to save your putrid, weak little soul.' His words rattled the air, as real as they were when he said them. The woman's expression unchanged; she didn't hear them. *Was she the sister and mother?* I could see her, interact with her yet she was alive.

"I don't know what you're talking about. Who are you? Why have you pulled me away from finding my daughter? Leave me alone!" A burst of inner strength surged forth and my words came out malevolently with an edge of echo, and light filled the air around me then slunk back.

Her mouth twisted to the side and she sighed. "Calm down. You will see her soon."

"Who are you?" I seethed, anger coiling around me like springs.

"Your aunt." The anger in me didn't faze her.

"I don't have one." Then the freesia scent in my mother's world returned and I remembered. I swallowed. "I did. She died years ago." White hot anger passed over me. This was not Aunt Carly, although there was a tiny resemblance.

Her eyebrows formed a V. "You know you're adopted?"

I nodded, my anger going from boiling to simmering. "My parents never kept that from me." *It was everything else.* Even as I thought that, I knew it was my fault too. I never wanted to know.

"So you met an aunt, one you were related to?"

Why was this any of her business? Her soothing voice calmed the beast in me fighting to get out and destroy everything. "Yes! She was my biological mother's paternal aunt. What does this have to do with anything?"

The wheels in her mind spun, I could see it in her eyes. She shook her head. "Nothing. When you reach the peaceful beyond, hopefully you will see her again."

Her words were more a question than a statement, but I ignored it. "Then what do you want?" Curiosity filled me. "How is it you can see me?"

She swallowed. "I'm your maternal aunt -- Scarlett. Your mother, Philmonia, was my half-sister. I was born with the ability to interact with spirits."

"I can't leave. My daughter. I have to save her." The anger gone and my voice now frantic.

"Your daughter is safe. I've taken great pains to see that she's cared for."

I shook my head. "You don't understand." The darkness swirling around Erica in my vision gave me a sense of urgency. "They're coming for her."

"They?" she asked, raising a platinum brow.

"Yes, the man from the shadowy vortex. I saw it. They want her." My purpose was becoming clearer.

That piqued her interest. She grabbed my hands and sent pictures into my mind. My brother, Evan, the one who destroyed my family, lay in a bed in a pool of his own blood. "That man?"

"No, he's... is he dead?" A sense of justice and relief washed over me. I'd never wish death on anyone, but was happy to see he got what he gave.

She nodded. "Yes, murdered the way he murdered. He can't get to Erica."

"It's not him. The man I saw was tall, blond, green eyes." I told her about the black vortex and the man's words saying I would meet his sister, our mother, when she tried to save my soul. I left out his ugliness.

"There are things you should know." She explained how her brother haunted her, killed people, and how my mother and her first husband impregnated her against her will, forcing her to have the baby. That baby was Evan. The man I thought was my biological brother. He wasn't. She trapped her brother's spirit in the child to free herself of him. She was eighteen, barely an adult. She had no idea their souls would bind, creating a monster. The green-eyed man from the vortex was her brother and son. Two souls trapped in one body. Now it made odd sense.

A part of me wanted to hate her, but I couldn't. It was my mother who deserved my hate. There was so much more to the story than I ever would have found out even if I'd asked the questions while I was alive. The skeletons in my family's closet were pieced together through the words and images she sent me.

"They want my daughter," I whispered.

"They can't have her." She swallowed. "It's time."

"Time for what?"

"To see your baby."

I stumbled over my words. "But how? I was almost..."

She raised her pointer finger to her mouth. "Shh... You don't have a physical form to slow you down. As a spirit, all you need to do is imagine being with her and you'll be there. Before you go," her eyes searched mine, "stay inside the house. It's safe there. Promise me." She held out her pinky.

I looped my pinky around hers. "I will."

"I'll see you soon."

I imagined the house and my little Erica and within a moment was inside the house watching my baby. Her curls bounced as she played with Mike, riding his back like a horse. He neighed and she giggled. Erica was happy and so were Mike and Lori. Tears of joy filled my eyes.

My vision of her and the dark shadows teeming around her stole the happiness I felt. Anxiety crept on me.

The woman, my aunt, had something up her sleeve. I saw it in her eyes. Blinking back the bad thoughts, I watched my baby laugh and play with her uncle.

The door opened, Lori walked in with a couple bags from *Cheeky Chicken*. They piled around the table, strapping Erica into a booster seat and placing an open box of chicken nuggets in front of her. She gouged them into the ketchup, double- and triple-dipping. When she was through with the nuggets she glanced towards me and smiled. Then she pointed and called, "Mommy!"

Mike and Lori turned their heads in unison but, unlike Erica, they looked through me. I slipped around the corner. *How could she see me? Was she like my aunt Scarlett, born with a gift to see and interact with ghosts?* That was crazy. I reminded myself that according to movies and TV children often saw spirits but grew out of it over time and never remembered being able to do it.

I stayed out of sight, watching from afar. When they put her to bed I waited until she was asleep and crawled onto the little toddler bed and curled beside her. She smelled fresh from her bath, her skin was soft as microfiber and I felt human in that moment.

"Mommy," said her little voice.
"Yes, baby."
"I love you. Are you stay me?"
I smiled and giggled at her improper sentence. She was getting so big, stringing words together now.
"As long as I can."
"OK."

For the next several days or weeks -- time worked different for me-- I watched my family and daughter. I could stay here forever. Mike was an excellent father and Lori a devoted mom. My daughter got lucky, just as I did. Watching them interact I understood why my parents never told me anything about my past. It would have ruined me and taken the smile off my face just as it would Erica's if she knew.

Every night I snuggled next to Erica's sweet form and watched her tiny chest rise and fall with each breath. Most nights I stayed next to her until morning came, watching over her like an angel, so when I saw a form outside her window, through the drawn curtains, I couldn't see it clearly. I left Erica's side to investigate.

Scarlett had warned me not to leave the house, not to go outside and I hadn't, but I couldn't have someone outside the house that would harm my family so with great trepidation I slipped outside the wall. Hands grabbed my shoulders from behind. The only hands that could touch me were ghosts.

"Sweetie, she's very cute isn't she?"

I recognized the voice of my mother and a strength I hadn't known when I was alive gripped me. This must be why Aunt Scarlett warned me about leaving the house. I wouldn't let anyone harm my baby. I threw my shoulders back, releasing her grip and turned. "What are you doing here?"

"You're my baby and belong with me."

All the horrible images of things my mother did roiled through my electrical impulses. I saw every moment and felt the pain she caused Scarlett and, no doubt, Evan. "I don't belong to you. I never did. Now go!" My red hot anger swelled as I shouted the words at her. She vanished and reappeared by my side.

"Not without you." She laced her fingers through mine. Her voice was syrupy.

I vanished, reappearing a few feet from her. Anger, might, courage throbbed, and a white light burst around me. I pointed. "Go!"

She faded, her bony fingers reaching for me as she disappeared into the darkness of the night. The light surrounding me curled and drew inside me.

Standing alone in their back yard I realized I had power inside me, a force that made her disappear, but for how long?

Chapter 34

Stones and Herbs

My little family took a trip to the park. Mike spread out the table cloth on the wooden bench table and unpacked their picnic lunch. Lori pushed Erica on the swings and helped her up the slide, catching her at the bottom. Erica's giggles gave me peace but I watched carefully for my mother and the ghost from the dark vortex.

"Are you ready?" Scarlett appeared at my side. I hadn't heard her walk up, as if her extra sight made her ghostly too.

"For what?"

"To enter the peaceful beyond?"

I didn't want to go. A nagging told me it wasn't time to go. I had a task to do. "No, I'm staying."

Instead of arguing she strolled towards my family, the edges of her skirt blowing in the breeze. A black object dropped from her hand as she stepped past their little picnic.

"Sigh, she never gives up." My mother stood beside me. Her fingers fanned out in front of her as she smoothed her fingernails.

I glared and seethed. "I banished you once. Why are you here?"

"Honey, you can't get rid of me that easy. You've been a ghost for, what? A year or so. I've been this way too long to remember. That white light trick is pretty unique." She giggled. "But not enough to send me away permanently." Her voice turned sinister.

I didn't have time for her silly talk. Keeping an eye focused on my family, Erica pointed at something on the grass. Lori stood, bent down and picked it up. The black object Scarlett dropped.

"No, I thought it was pretty unique too." I mocked my mother then allowed angry energy to surge and banished her again. White light spread out and sucked her in. I wasn't sure it would work again and sighed when it did. That was one problem gone now.

I moved closer as Lori handed Scarlett the black object.

"She can keep it. I have several." Scarlett raised her arm, her sleeve dropped to her shoulder revealing an assortment of bracelets.

"No, we can't." Lori held her hand with the object in it between her and Scarlett.

"I insist." Scarlett closed her hand around the object. "It has special qualities that bring peace to the one wearing it. Of course, that's just silly hocus pocus. I'd like her to keep it."

Lori drew her hand back and gave her a cynical smile. "Sure. Thank you." She dropped it in her pocket.

A few clouds blotted out the sun. I appeared at Scarlett's side. "What is that thing you gave my daughter?"

"It's a bracelet made of stones that will keep evil spirits away. Your daughter needs to wear it."

Lori put it in her pocket. How was I going to get it out? Knowing Lori, she'd toss it. If it did what

Scarlett said, Erica needed it. Scarlett walked beneath the trees and parked on a wooden bench. "How?"

"That's your job."

Erica! She could see me! The sun reappeared through the clouds and I reappeared at Erica's side. "Mommy, Mommy!" she called.

I lifted a finger to my mouth. "Shh."

She chuckled. Mike opened a box drink and handed it to Erica. She sipped. "Peabudder, jowwy." Lori placed a PB & J sandwich on a paper plate along with a handful of strawberries.

Blackness covered the park. I lifted my head to the sky. It was going to downpour. Mike and Lori continued to eat as if a major storm wasn't dwelling in the clouds above them. I glanced at the kids on the playground, other families barbecuing, laughing, playing ball, not one of them was in a rush to seek cover.

The blackness took over the park then shrunk, hovering in the sky above my family. Tentacles spread out from the thick, dark cloud in three different directions. They took on the form of three separate orbs and sped towards my family.

Erica! They were after her. The shadowy forms that surrounded my daughter in the vision. It was happening! The bracelet. "Erica." She glanced at me. "Get the bracelet from Aunt Lori's pocket. You must get the bracelet." My voice was frantic. The black orbs moved closer each second.

Erica looked away from me and to Lori. "Mommy says I need bacelet, Lowi."

Lori and Mike's eyes met for a split second then Lori's brows lowered. She'd already made up her mind not to give Erica the bracelet from the stranger. Now wasn't the time! *Damnit, stop being such a freaking awesome mom and give her the fucking bracelet!*

She set her sandwich down. "We don't accept gifts from strangers."

"Mommy not a stranger. Mommy here. She says it OK." I couldn't help but smile listening to my little girl's speech. She was speaking so well. That moment didn't last long. The dark orbs were moving closer.

I scanned the park for Scarlett but didn't see her anywhere. She'd left me alone. Could she see the orbs? They were low enough now they spun around the table.

Erica shuddered, her eyes searching the orbs as they enveloped the table. "I'm scared, Mommy." Her bright blue eyes pleaded to me. I had to protect her, so I wrapped my body around hers. They weren't taking her.

"Why not give it to her?" Mike asked.

The orbs coalesced into a single ball and elongated into the form of a small person. Lori twisted her mouth. "I don't know, Mike."

Give her the fucking bracelet! Darkness moved away from the form, leaving a small child.

Chapter 35

Progeny

The child's straight brown hair rested against her shoulders, blue eyes stared from under her bangs. She moved closer. "Scarlett, where are you? What's happening?" I called, but the woman didn't appear. I couldn't leave Erica. I had to figure this out.

Erica beamed. "Want a stawbewwy?" She held out a fat one in her hand.

The little girl from the orbs smiled as she stepped towards her. She appeared as an innocent child, but she wasn't. I didn't think anyone else saw her as they didn't pay her any mind, not even Mike or Lori. No parent called for her. She was a spirit, a dark spirit, with a face of innocence sent to trick my child. "Don't talk to her, sweetie."

Erica eyed me curiously. "She my fend."

"No, she's not your friend," I corrected, my face stern.

Water pooled in Erica's eyes, making me feel as big as a flea.

"Who are you talking to?" asked Lori, her face filled with concern.

Erica glanced up at her. "Mommy and my fend." The words came out as if everything was normal and everyone could see spirits.

The little orb child moved closer, her cherub face and pudgy cheeks were a ploy. I concentrated my energy working into anger and courage. I still hadn't figured out exactly how it worked, and since blasting my mother, didn't know if I'd expended too much of it, but I had to try.

The orb child stood only inches from my baby. She held out her hand. Erica reached out. "No, baby. No!" I swatted at her hand but mine went through hers.

The orb girl ran off towards the woods. Erica jumped off the bench, sinking through my arms, and chased the little girl.

"I'll get her," Mike said as if he was in a tunnel and chased after her. They disappeared beneath the trees.

Chapter 36

Labyrinth

I followed them into the woods. The trees disappeared and walls built up around me forming corridors. Flames flickered from invisible sconces on the walls. "Erica!" *Where was she?*

In a frenzy, I flew up and down the corridors, lost in the maze. A room appeared in front of me, a light shone on a blond child curled into the fetal position, crying and holding her blanket. "Erica?" The child lifted her head and I gasped. It wasn't Erica, but me. Footfalls, abrupt and distinct, pounded the ground, rattling the walls and causing the flames to bounce. I turned and stepped backwards. I wasn't floating anymore. My feet touched the ground and I pressed my hand against the wall. It didn't go though.

That wasn't possible. I was a ghost now and had no physical form in the world. As I sought to understand, a man emerged. I recognized him from the green truck so many years ago. A sinister grin ground into his face. He stood motionless, not in contemplation but premeditation. When he opened his mouth laughter, malevolent laughter, erupted.

His face melted and my mother took his spot. "Did your light burn out, honey?" she asked, in a sarcastic tone, a sneer painted on her face.

My light? My light, that was it. I needed to find it and banish the spirits. Her face melted away, as had the man's, and was replaced by Evan's. Flame shadows bounced across his bald head and his blue eyes widened. Clouds of black swirled and covered the irises completely, even the white. I stepped back, reaching for the baby me, but she was gone. Evan vanished and I was alone.

Something soft brushed against my leg. The orb girl stared up at me. Her blue eyes pleading as she reached for my hand. I snapped it back. Tears welled in the corners of her eyes. "Mommy."

"Erica. Where are you, honey?"

"I'm wight hee-we."

Frantic, I turned, searching for her. "Where, honey?"

"Wight hee-we." A small hand grabbed mine.

The orb child had wrapped her hand around a couple of my fingers. "Erica?"

"Mommy."

The child's mouth didn't move. It wasn't her. She wasn't my Erica. I knelt and met her at eye level. "Erica?"

"I not Erica. I love Erica." She wrapped her hands around my neck. I wrapped my arms around the child and smoothed her silky, dark hair.

"Where's Erica, sweetie?"

The child vanished from my arms without another word, replaced by nothing. I dropped my head in defeat and cried into my arms.

The still air suddenly eddied around me like air trapped in a walkway. Leaves spiraled with it and

Erica appeared in the center. "Erica." I reached for her but the spinning winds burned my arms like scraping an open wound on carpet. Shadows ascended from the ground, joining the leaves in rotation around my daughter. I pushed my way into the whirling mess. The shadows moved through my translucent body and I jolted backwards, hitting the wall.

Anger twined itself around me like a vine. *They couldn't have my baby!* A scream pierced the air before I realized it was my own and light spilled from me. The darkness gone, replaced by streams of pure energy. The walls of the corridors broke and crumbled, eventually falling away in dust. Streams of light continued to surge.

"Emily!" a voice called from somewhere inside the light. "Emily!"

Scarlett's face appeared, her hair nearly matching the color of the light burning from me. I'd turned into a ghostly flashlight.

In her hand was a tiny hand. The child's other hand was positioned over her squinted eyes. "Erica!" I dropped to my knees and folded her into my arms.

"You bwight," she stated in a profound voice.

"Erica!" Mike's voice called in a panic. Leaves and dirt crunched beneath his feet as he searched for my child.

"Over here," Scarlett called and tugged Erica's hand. "Let's find your Uncle Mike."

"OK." She tugged me. "Mommy coming."

Scarlett led her by the hand without answering her question. I dropped back as I watched my beautiful living baby walk away from me.

Mike turned the corner, his face a mess of wrinkles and fear. The moment he saw her, relief fell over his expression. He grabbed her and swirled her in his strong arms and tucked her head against his shoulder. "I love you so much. Don't ever run off again."

Another set of footfalls crunched the leaves and Lori appeared, joining the family bear hug.

They thanked Scarlett profusely. My baby was in good hands. Mike and Lori would soon be the only parents she knew. Memories of me would slip from her mind, but all that was OK, because my little girl would always be loved by my older brother and best friend. An unlikely family emerged from the trees. Erica riding her uncle's shoulders.

Chapter 37

A Peace of Death

The smile hadn't left Scarlett's face as she stood beside me, watching my family pack up their picnic and head to the car. Lori glanced back at her after tucking Erica carefully into her car seat, waved, then pulled a black object out of her pocket. The bracelet; only, Erica didn't need it anymore. I was still glad to know she'd be wearing it.

"Are you ready?"

Scarlett's words pulled me away from my thoughts as their SUV backed up and pulled away from the parking lot. I sighed. "Is a ghost ever ready?"

She glanced down then met my gaze. "You aren't an ordinary ghost. I've never seen any do what you did."

"Ghost powers must run in the family like extrasensory perception. Mine didn't kick in until I died." I laughed nervously.

Her lip turned up in a quirky smile and she bit her bottom lip. "There may be more truth to that than you know." Her words drifted off and I swore I heard her think, *If only you knew.*

I didn't care. There was nothing more about my demented biological family I needed to know. I saved my daughter, and that's all that mattered. That's why I hadn't moved into the *peaceful beyond* when I died.

Debbie
Evan's Girls Book 3
Part 1
Gifted

Chapter 1

Dimwit

My earliest memory is the scent of my mother. She smells like gardenias in full bloom. I inhale deeply, as if it will help me remember better, but there are no gardenias here. I see her smile, teeth straight and white, her lips red as cherries. The sun on her ebony skin makes it glow and her eyes are like dark silk. I know most of that is a fabrication in my head, since I was a baby when she died.

A breeze rustles the leaves hanging from the cypress. My mind sees them sway. When I open my eyes, they hang still, Spanish moss falling over the edges like a waterfall. I wonder if my mother sat beneath the same trees and imagined life. I often sneak away, whenever I think I won't get caught.

My mother grew up in the house I live in. It's large, with four columns in front as if they're holding it up. The porch wraps around it. Inside is a large entryway with fine marble floors that have seen better days. There are many rooms. I should know, as I spend days exploring.

The staircase loops around with iron bars. Glass chandeliers hang from the high ceiling and fancy designs are carved into the molding around the walls, floors and walkways, and ceiling. There's the library filled with rows of books and a ladder that rolls along the shelves to reach the high ones.

There are large windows in each room of the house. Light spills through, casting its radiance, except in the library; because of its burgundy walls and dark wood, it always looks like night. At one time the home was marvelous, but now it is in need of paint and repairs.

My uncle is a shrewd man who misers every penny and my aunt walks around with a chip on her shoulder. Neither like me much. They don't say it in words, but they do in actions and expressions. I'm not their child. I'm not even a child they wanted in their home. They took me in because there was no one else and they hide me away. I haven't seen beyond our lonely spot in the bayou.

The crunching of dirt alerts me someone is near. Judging by the steps, it's Malery, my disgruntled cousin. A kick to my thigh tells me I was right. "Hey dimwit, where the fuck you been?"

I cringed. I hated that name -- dimwit -- because my mother was black and he, like the rest of my family, considered people with color stupid. Although it was better than the other names he's called me over the years. "I have a name, you know."

He shrugged. "Whatever. Get the fuck back home."

He kicked the dirt beside my head. The particles blew in my face. I sat up, spitting the dirt from my lips. Luckily, I closed my eyes in time. He meant business. If I didn't follow him now I'd get the attic. It was filled with shadows that crept in the dark and loud moans and creaks. It was there I found the locket. It was hung on a long gold chain with a skeleton key. One side was a beautiful young woman with skin the color of mine. I imagined it was my mom, but I really didn't know.

Malery stayed two steps behind me, kicking the dirt every few feet so it would spray on my legs. I didn't say a word, but imagined kicking dirt clods into his eyes and pouring mud over his head. I touched the locket under my shirt. To me, it was a way of keeping my mom close, even though I knew she probably wasn't my mom. It didn't matter, because if she was alive I wouldn't be here in this shipwreck of a mansion living with a wretched family.

I opened the door and was greeted by my aunt. "Where have you been?" she sneered. "I told you not to leave the grounds. If you can't follow the rules I'll put a chain leash around that ankle." She kicked my shin for emphasis.

I cringed, but knew better than to speak. She was mean enough to act on her words. I ate my dinner at the small table in the kitchen by myself. They always ate in the dining room, but I wasn't allowed to join them. I wasn't allowed out of my room when they had company. I dared not try, or it would be the attic with the ghosts.

After dinner, I cleaned the dishes and packed away the leftovers. From the window of my room, I stared at the moon. It was a full, blood-red moon. A gunshot cracked through the sky, shaking the house to its foundation.

Chapter 2

Shadow Man

Shattered glass and a loud thunk followed the gunshot. I jolted upright and rushed to the stairs, stopping at the banister and ogling the sight below. The foyer window was shot out and glass surrounded my uncle as he lay on the ground, blood spilling around him. I walked slowly down the stairs to see his face. It wasn't my uncle. I didn't know the man. His square jaw hung limp and he was thinner around the middle.

"What are you doing out here?" my aunt snapped.

The man disappeared and my aunt stood at the bottom of the steps. A scowl on her face, hands on her hips.

"I thought I heard something." My voice was tiny as I labored each word from my mouth. I glanced again at the spot where the man lay. The dull marble floor stared back at me, void of anything but dust.

My aunt's eyes narrowed. "Get back to your room."

She didn't need to say it twice. I turned tail and ran up the steps.

The next morning Miss Dresdan came by. She was the only person outside the home I spoke with and that was only because she tutored me while she cared for my grandmother, who was very ill. I didn't doubt she was sworn to secrecy to never reveal I lived here. I didn't understand why, and often wondered what the world was like outside the bayou.

Part of my studies was reading a book a week. In them I traveled to other places and became someone other than myself. Her voice comforted me, but today was different. There was something wrong. I heard it in her shaky voice. Instead of going downstairs as usual, I hunkered against the wall near the iron banister, listening to Miss Dresdan.

"Something horrible, just horrible, happened last night. Mr. Aimes was shot. The bullet went right through the window." She cupped her hands over her rosy cheeks. Her eyes shifted to the stairs, as if she knew I was there. Strands of golden hair strayed from the bun on her head.

"That is horrible. How is his wife?" my aunt responded, her voice lacking any emotion.

"Oh, Mrs. James, she's beside herself. Hasn't spoken since she found him."

A gunshot, glass, and a dead man. *Is that what I saw?*

"What the fuck you doing on the ground?" Malery spat as he walked towards me.

I grabbed my foot and tugged at my shoe, pulling my legs in at the same time, anticipating the kick. "It feels like a sticker is in my shoe."

"Whatever." He slugged his backpack over his shoulder and walked by without kicking my leg or shin. Today I was spared. My legs bore bruises in a variety of colors, depending on their stage of healing. I stood and watched him stalk past my aunt and Miss Dresdan to the front door.

"Grab some breakfast," my aunt ordered.

"I don't have time. I'll miss the bus," he grumbled back.

She sneered. "I said grab some breakfast."

He let out a breath. "Fine!" Then stomped to the kitchen.

I crept down the stairs and walked past my aunt and Miss Dresdan. Their conversation changed and they were discussing my grandmother.

She was very ill or really old, I didn't know which and, at that time, took them for the same thing. I was only eight and two-thirds years old.

When I reached the spot I'd seen the man, the image came to me again. My mind replayed it. My guts cringed at the bloody sight. Last night it looked real. Today, the image was faded and see-through. It had really happened.

I finished my math and got settled into a chair to read. My escape from the horrible reality of my life.

A hand gently touched my head and a finger raked through my coily hair. "We need to do something about this hair." Miss Dresdan dropped onto her knees and grabbed my hands. "And I brought just the thing." She winked.

I adored her. She was the only person in my life that treated me as a person, except my grandmother. I wasn't allowed in her room, so I didn't really know if she liked me or not. I'd seen her from the doorway. Her skin was pale as paper, her hair dark as a raven. They were a contrast to each other. I imagined when she was young she must have been very beautiful.

Miss Dresdan pulled a brush from her bag and a couple bottles. She sat on the edge of the bed. "Come sit in front of me."

I did. She sprayed my hair and ran the brush through my coils that sprang back the second the brush released them. She grabbed another bottle and squished gel stuff into her hand then pulled it though my hair, massaging my head as she went. The motions relaxed me.

"Take a look." She held an oval mirror with worn gold filigree around the edges in front of me. "You are such a beautiful girl."

She'd placed my hair in two ponytails. Each coil separated with care, hanging in spirals that rested above my shoulders. I rarely did anything with my hair and hadn't realized how long it was. A few stray coils rested against my forehead and cheeks, purposely placed there.

I stared with wide eyes. The bands holding the ringlets had red dragonflies on the attachments that were see through like stained glass.

She leaned in and whispered in my ear, "What's eating at you today?"

"Nothing," I retorted quickly.

She sat behind me with her face next to mine. "How about we go for a walk?"

I nodded.

The muggy air hung around us as we walked towards the trees, towards the bayou. Spanish moss and lush greenery enveloped us and blocked the sun's rays but didn't stop the air from feeling as though it was suffocating each breath I took.

She held my hand. "It's really beautiful here."

I nodded but didn't say a word.

We neared my area, the place I laid under the trees and visited my mother, if only in my head. I wasn't permitted to go further, so when she continued walking I froze.

She turned. "What's wrong?"

"You know."

She smiled. "It's OK, you're with me."

Reluctantly, knowing if I got caught it would be the attic with or without her, I continued, my hand still in hers.

"You heard us this morning didn't you?"

I nodded, confused as to where this conversation was going.

"That's why you didn't come down immediately."

I nodded again, my guts knotting up.

She stopped just before the walking bridge. "It's OK." She searched my face and, as if she could read my mind, said, "Did you know?"

"Know what?"

"About Mr. Aimes?"

I shook my head. "How would I know? I don't even know him."

"It's OK. This place holds magic and some people are touched by it."

"What does that mean?"

"That some people have gifts and I think you're one of them."

I furrowed my brows. "Gifts?"

"One day, you'll go far away from here. A place where it's OK to be you." The conversation took a 180. "I'm just over the bridge. Now, hurry home before anyone knows you've gone too far."

Chapter 3

Lonely Cupcake

That was the day I realized I saw things others didn't. The visions came when I least expected them and left without a trace.

Thunder rumbled through the sky and buckets of rain splattered against the window. Lights dotted the bayou in contrast to the darkness of my life, when all at once they blinked off. Someone closed the lid on the watery hole with us inside it.

I closed the drapes and settled into my bed, drawing the covers over my head. When I opened my eyes next, sunlight streamed through the white sheers. It was my tenth birthday. There were no birthday wishes or cake. No presents, but that day found a way to define my childhood.

I sat at the small table in the kitchen eating my breakfast, a bowl of oatmeal, when Miss Dresdan entered. "Good morning!" she stated with a delightful smile.

"Good morning," I echoed as she rushed into the next room. Through the walls I heard muffled conversation between Miss Dresdan and my aunt.

In my room, I worked quietly on my studies, my eyes preoccupied as they stared out the window. The cypress rose from the placid water, leaves swaying in the light breeze. Flowers in bloom splashed color everywhere, meaning spring had arrived. It was the season I liked the most, everything was green and bright.

"Debbie!" my aunt called from the bottom of the steps, her voice carrying more anger than usual.

I jumped from my seat and rushed to the stairs, my heart palpitating in fear. I stopped cold. She stood at the bottom of the steps, her mouth in a downward curve, eyebrows lifted, and forehead wrinkled. "Get down here now!"

I swallowed hard and slowly took each step.

"Do I need to drag you? Get your ass down the stairs."

The anger in her voice boomed in my head. One minute I was lost in the tranquility outside, now I was thrust into the chaos inside. I picked up my pace until I was standing in front of her. She grabbed my ear and dragged me into the kitchen.

When we reached the sink she let go and pointed. "Is this what you call cleaning the kitchen?" Pools of water were splashed over the counter and dribbled into a puddle on the floor.

"No, ma'am. I'm sorry." It didn't matter that I hadn't done it. When I left the kitchen the breakfast dishes were done and the counter neatly wiped. No. It was Malery. I didn't have to witness him in action to know. He found whatever means necessary to make my life a living hell.

"You'll clean it up then you will go outside and pull the weeds around the hedges." She huffed as she exited the room.

Pulling weeds wasn't the worst as it gave me time to enjoy the spring day when there was enough breeze to blow away some of the humidity. Bees hummed and buzzed around the azaleas as I sat on the grass and grabbed at the weeds, my mind a million miles away.

"What are you doing?" asked a girl's voice that startled me from my thoughts.

I turned to see a girl about my age. Her smile grabbed my attention because her teeth were so white they gleamed in the sun surrounded by pink lips and full cheeks.

She sat on the ground next to me. "My name is Noela." She cocked her head. "You don't say much."

Insects crawled along the tract of my intestines as I tried to think of something to say. *Was she real? Where did she come from?* If I spoke to her, what punishment would my aunt bestow on me?

"You don't have to talk. I will." She yanked at a clump of weeds and plunked them down on my stack.

"I just moved here. I don't have any friends yet."

We continued pulling weeds for several more minutes before I spoke. "Debbie."

Her face lit up like fireworks over the bayou. "That wasn't so hard was it?" she joked, leaning into me. "Maybe you can show me around?"

I glanced over my shoulder to be sure my aunt wasn't somewhere watching, waiting to find me in the forbidden act of interacting with the outside world. "Maybe." I closed my eyes in apprehension of something; a slap on my face, tug at my ear, the threat of the attic, but nothing happened.

"You're a silly girl. I have to get home before my dad comes looking. Can we meet later?"

I opened my mouth to speak, but no words came out. I wanted nothing more than to meet her later and run through the trees, take someone to my special, magic spot where my mother joined me but... The shadow of my family hung over me like a dark cloud in a thunderstorm. "I don't think so," finally spilled from my mouth.

"OK, maybe tomorrow?"

She was persistent, so I nodded.

"I live through there." She pointed towards the far, woody side of the property. "If you walk straight you'll find my house. Meet you halfway." She pulled herself off the ground. "See you tomorrow, Debbie."

That was it and she was gone. I watched as she ran through the trees and listened until I no longer heard the brush of leaves or patter of her feet.